14

Beneath Buddha's Eyes

Beneath Buddha's Eyes

Tony Anthony

Welcome Rain Publishers
NEW YORK

Beneath Buddha's Eyes
Copyright © 2002 by Tony Anthony.
All rights reserved.

Library of Congress CIP data available from the publisher.

Direct any inquiries to
Welcome Rain Publishers LLC

ISBN 1-56649-252-1

Printed in the United States of America by
HAMILTON PRINTING COMPANY

Interior design and composition by
MULBERRY TREE PRESS, INC.
(www.mulberrytreepress.com)

First Edition: November 2002
1 3 5 7 9 10 8 6 4 2

There is no cure for death.

—Gautama Buddha

For Monika

1

It was 2:45 A.M. and Peter Hill reached over to switch on the lamp beside the bed. He pulled the covers down from his forehead, opened his eyes, and stared up at the ceiling, terrified. Then he focused his eyes on the foot of the bed. Otherwise, he knew the dream would grow and become too real, too overpowering. He had plenty of experience with these dreams. They almost always took place in the jungle, running like movie reels on the screen behind his eyelids. Sometimes they played in black and white, where odd and sickening shapes manifested themselves out of the black empty space between the trees. Shapes that really had no meaning—nothing he'd ever remembered seeing—just pure fright, pure horror, in 3D. Sometimes the reel would be in color so saturated and bright it hurt the eyes to witness it. Often in the color reels, there would be people and places he recognized. Once he'd been a young boy selling Coca-Colas to a platoon of American GIs. The bottles were warm and as the soldiers began to drink, their heads puffed up until they were bigger than a house. Their grotesque-looking heads finally exploded, blowing him backward into the jungle, so he rolled over and over with each blast of wind from an exploding head suffocating him like a horrible-smelling fart.

He'd played hundreds of these reels as if he had been a projectionist who never left the movie house to go out into the light of day. Sometimes he thought of just staying in bed under the covers—never, ever climbing out into the world's harsh reality.

The light woke Nina up. She pushed herself up, leaning back against the headboard, and looked down at him.

"What is it?"

"I was on the Ho Chi Minh Trail."

"Again?"

2

Up on Trimmingham's pond, in the far north corner of the small village of East Millbank, Connecticut, where Peter and Nina lived with their two young boys, it was still dark. It was summer, before dawn. The wind blew through the trees, but the water was calm.

The pond stood perfectly still. It was like a pool of black india ink whose edge began a few inches in front of Peter's boots. Puffs of wind pushed through the tops of the trees. He listened to a field mouse rustle the leaves on the ground.

Peter was lost within this solitary realm that was as much in his imagination as in the world—this great space like an invisible room in the quiet woods . . .

A solitary puff of wind brushed across his face. He listened to the whir of his fishing reel, then the plunk of the Silver Flier.

He looked down at the angry face that stared back at him from the surface of the pond. There in the dark water, reflected beneath the brim of his red wool cap, was the deep frown he'd grown used to seeing each morning in the shaving mirror. Above the pond, the last clouds of night were like black strokes of paint on an artist's canvas. A quick puff of breeze ran its cool hand through the trees, causing a shiver to run up his spine. Yet the pond remained still, its fragile mirrored surface broken only by the plunk of the Silver Flier. He watched the small concentric circles

grow wider and wider until they fanned out across the entire surface of
the pond, lapping softly against the shore. He reeled in the lure watching it twist and turn like a shimmering jewel swimming toward him just
beneath the surface of the water. The breeze brushed across his face and
the backs of his hands. Peter was keenly aware of every inch of his surroundings. Nothing escaped him. It was there, in the middle of the kind
heart of nature, where he felt at home. He reeled in the Silver Flier
watching the nylon line draw a path through the water. So clean, so simple. He kept his attention on the fishing, careful not to let his thoughts
stray, his mind swimming with the trout he knew were hiding a few feet
beneath the surface of the pond. He had learned not to let the memories
intrude. As soon as he felt one about to begin, he'd lock it out. He
thought they couldn't be considered real anymore. He wasn't even sure
which ones might be true and which were not. So he'd cast out the Silver Flier again and listen for the comforting plunk.

From far off—six, maybe seven miles—he heard the heavy rotor blades
of a helicopter beating out their rhythm against the cool morning air. It
was unmistakably a Huey, the kind of chopper that carried him to and
from the field in Nam. Suddenly he forgot about the fishing. He let the
line go limp—the string settling on the surface of the water in a long S.
He listened for the helicopter like a deer listening for a predator. He
could hear every nuance of the Huey's sound. At about two miles from
where he stood, the pilot was decreasing the pitch on the blades, dropping to about a hundred feet above the ground. He knew it was low-lev-
eling, just above the treetops, because he could hear the engine noise
being absorbed by the trees. For several seconds its sound almost disappeared. He prepared himself, focusing his eyes at the point across the
pond where it would appear. He was dead on. He watched the chopper's
prop wash blast the leaves on the tops of the tall maples and oaks. His
head tracked back on his neck, his eyes riveted on the Huey. He fixed the
image in his mind like a snapshot. It roared across the pond in only a split
second. But he saw the skids, the skew of the stern rotor, the hook on the

bottom, even the expression on the pilot's face. The chopper flew so low he could feel the heat from the engine settle on his face as it passed. It blew him away. Suddenly his legs went weak. He sat back on the damp ground listening to the noise of the chopper echo off the pond after it had passed. Even after the sound was gone, he could hear it in his head. He had to remind himself that he was in East Millbank, Connecticut. For christsakes, he knew this.

But he wasn't able to escape the power the Huey had over him. He held his head in his hands. He wanted to cry but knew he wouldn't.

3

"Peter, your descriptions are wonderful," said his therapist. "I feel I'm there. I can hear the sounds, smell the smells."

Peter was in therapy out of desperation, when drinking didn't work anymore. He had been yelling at everyone—mostly at his wife, Nina, and his young sons, especially Mathew. When Peter yelled, it made the awful sound in his head go away.

One day he found himself standing in his front hall, towering over five-year-old Mathew, screaming down at him as he cowered on the doormat. Looking down at his beautiful young son, Peter was scared—he'd forgotten why he was yelling. He had no idea what Mathew could've done to cause such a horrible reaction. He felt like he'd fallen over the edge of a cliff into some sort of void. He felt completely lost, empty, floating endlessly down . . .

There were three nearly identical white-clapboard colonial houses sitting one beside the other, just north of town. They seemed to be gazing solemnly out at Main Street. Their identical white picket fences were joined, like friendly neighbors shaking hands, along the sidewalk. The one farthest to the north belonged to a young stockbroker he'd said hello to only once. The next belonged to the Franklins, an elderly couple, descended from of one of East Millbank's founders. Mr. Franklin had been

Peter's milkman when he was growing up. The third was nearly identical except for the presence of a small wooden sign that hung to the right of the front door. Gold-leafed letters carved into a solid piece of cherry spelled out, GISELLA GRUN, PH.D.

Gisella sat across from Peter in her office, uncrossing, then crossing her long legs. He could tell she was unaware she was playing with a few straggling blond hairs hanging over her ear. Her hair was short, which might have made her seem cold were it not for the compassion in her intense sky-blue eyes.

Gisella was forty-five. They were the same age. Peter sometimes found himself attracted to Gisella, but she was careful to cut off any feelings that might surface between them. She was the one person on earth who gave Peter hope of finding his way through the maze of memories— some half remembered and most forgotten—about Vietnam. They'd been walking the trail together, which is the way he thought of it, twice a week for almost three years. There was nothing he held back from Gisella. She knew every intimate detail of his life. It was because nothing remained hidden that he felt safe in her presence. And though he resigned himself to the fact that their relationship was going to remain doctor and patient, it made him happy to know more about Gisella than she thought he did. He knew her in secret ways—on subtler levels than she could ever imagine—from the way her thin body folded into his when they hugged after their sessions. When he held her, even if for just a few seconds, he could feel her muscles relax. He knew without doubt that she felt as safe in his arms as he did in hers.

Peter looked far younger than the other vets Gisella saw. His hair was still the same dark brown it had been in Vietnam apart from a few flecks of gray above the ears. He was over six feet tall and had remained fit by running five miles a day—even his drinking hadn't stopped him from running. Secretly, Gisella found him handsome in a brooding, dark sort of way.

Peter felt her eyes on him as he stood in her office in front of the bay window. Pressing his forehead against the cold windowpane, he held his hands up against the glass like a caged animal. He stared out at the lawn in front of the house, at the rain falling on the grass. He could see the blades moving. It looked like the rain was playing them as if they were the keys of some sort of exotic musical instrument.

"The weird thing is, I don't even remember her name." The window fogged up from his breath. "Katherine or Katy or . . . or . . . I just don't know. I think she was killed eventually."

He traced the letters K-A-T-E on the fogged glass with his finger. Then he backed away to gain some distance from the word he'd spelled out.

"Her name?" Gisella asked him.

"I don't remember her face."

"Tell me what you do remember."

"I was with her on the beach. We spent the morning swimming in the South China Sea."

It was difficult to dive back twenty-five years into his mind files, the ones he'd closed so long ago and locked under "Vietnam."

"The water was so full of phosphorescence that when she swam in front of me her kicks left footprints in the water." He turned to Gisella "You see?"

He walked to the black leather couch against the wall facing the window.

"Go on."

"God, this is too much . . . I see it now it's like a movie . . . I haven't seen this movie in such a long time." He fell back onto the couch, exhausted.

Gisella waited a minute, then said, "Tell me what you see."

"Her legs kicking. Her body made a tunnel in the phosphorescence. I swam through the tunnel . . ." He pushed himself up off the couch. He felt he needed to return to the window where the image of the word KATE had mostly faded and wipe away what was left.

"I was trying to be part of her life."

"In some way you wanted to get inside her?" Gisella uncrossed her legs.

He turned to look at Gisella, "No, that's not what I meant." He felt a frown etch itself into his forehead. "We had snorkels and masks on. Everything was crystal clear. We swam along a wall of coral." He turned to look out the window. "There was this giant shark. We startled him."

He paused, closing his eyes to watch the film again on the screen behind his eyelids. "You know what I remember?"

Gisella shook her head even though Peter wasn't looking at her.

"Kate didn't swim away. She stayed and watched the shark circle. I remember how the shark looked at her. It was very close to her. She could have touched it. Then, after a while when he was finished, he just swam away."

Peter walked back to the couch and sat down slowly. "There's something else. Later that day a soldier was killed by a shark. In that same spot."

He slumped down again, exhausted.

Gisella broke the silence. "It might be good for you to search for more clues about Kate's life. It might help you to dive deeper. You could start with the newspaper files at the library. After all, she was a civilian reporter. It would have been news." Gisella stopped for a moment, tucking the stray strands of hair away behind her ear. "This may be difficult for you, Peter."

When the session had ended and he walked across the gravel driveway to his Jeep, he felt both elated and exhilarated, heading like he was into new territory. He remembered having the same feeling heading into the boonies in Nam. When he drove down Gisella's driveway, listening to the gravel scrunch beneath his tires, he admitted to himself that he felt afraid. He sensed the journey could lead, as some of the bad trails had, into minefields. What he wanted to do at that very moment was to find a dark and quiet barroom—a safe place—in which to hide. But he knew he couldn't, if only because of the promise he'd made to Gisella at the outset of his therapy: He promised not to drink while he went through the process.

4

Peter sat at the microfiche machine in the East Millbank Library scrolling through *The New York Times* for 1968 and 1969, amazed at how old-fashioned the advertisements seemed. The styles of clothes, the automobiles. Names that had been lost in his memory for years passed by on the screen: General William Westmoreland, Secretary of State Henry Kissinger, President Richard Nixon. Peter knew just how fragile memories were, having seen so many so easily lost. He stopped at a page dated April 21, 1969. A headline on page 17 read, UPI CORRESPONDENT REPORTED DEAD IN VIETNAM. He scrolled down the article, reading as he went, until a picture of a woman appeared. His heart pounded in his chest. The face on the screen had such intensity it was impossible to look away. There was no hint of softness. Her eyes looked out from the large screen as if she was daring the world to see just how strong a woman could be. Or perhaps just how hard a war can turn a heart. She had the short hair of a man and she wore standard government-issue fatigues, but there in the grainy photograph was a beautiful woman, the woman Peter struggled to remember. Beneath the photo was the United Press International byline and the name "Katherine P. White."

Peter was transfixed. So many emotions ran through him he felt his face change expressions a dozen times in the space of a few seconds. He smiled. Grew sad. Then confused. He smiled again. His cheeks began twitching. He rubbed a hand across his forehead as if that could calm his thoughts. He sighed. Finally, he burst out crying. He'd come home. When he'd finally been pushed back far enough into the depths of his fragile heart, he felt like he'd just ended a long journey. He felt a huge relief, although he sensed a new journey was just beginning.

A white-haired man missing an arm stared at Peter over the top of his magazine. Although he felt embarrassed, Peter couldn't stop crying. He felt as if he'd torn a huge hole in a dam inside himself. The water rushed out all at once, and there was no stopping it. His sobs grew so strong they echoed off the library walls. Peter tried to guess why the old man watched so intently. He wondered if the man might have been a veteran of another war.

5

Hidden well off the road between Quang Ngai and Kontum in a makeshift prisoner-of-war camp, Kate White lay facedown in the mud with her hands tied behind her back. She held her face in a stagnant puddle of reddish brown water and though it smelled like shit, she took in huge gulps. A North Vietnamese soldier grasped her short brown hair jerking her head from the water.

"*Dung lai!* No more to drink!"

She turned her head and stared at the soldier before she gulped more of the brown water.

"*Mau len!* No more water! Hurry! Officer wants to meet American reporter."

"I told you, I'm not American, I'm Australian!"

The soldier pulled Kate onto her feet. Although soaked and undernourished, she was still quite beautiful—tall with deeply tanned skin and a confident look in her green eyes. The soldier led her into a bamboo hut where an NVA major stood straight as a stick of bamboo interrogating Kate's UPI bureau chief, Randall Guest. Randy was heavyset with three days' growth of silver stubble on his face. With his arms tied behind his back, he kneeled uncomfortably at the major's feet. Randy looked like a man who'd seen everything; even so, he was not at all comfortable in his present situation. The major signaled a soldier to lead Randy out, just as Kate was led in. The soldier pushed her onto her knees, where she took Randy's place on the floor. For Kate's benefit, the major lowered his eyes until they fell on the old mud-spattered Nikon F camera lying at his feet. Then as dramatically as if he'd seen it in an old French film, he pulled a French Gitane from his shirt pocket and lit it up without offering one to the prisoner he was trying to impress. With his head enveloped in a cloud of heavy blue smoke, he feigned interest as Kate began to speak.

"I'm a British subject, I demand to speak to my consulate."

The major smiled, picking up Kate's passport off the floor. "So it seems, Miss Katherine White. Anyone with some money can obtain one of these on the black market. Where do you live?"

"Sydney, Australia."

"In Vietnam!"

"In Saigon . . . mostly. I travel all over the country."

"So it seems. You speak the language?"

"I've been here four years. So I understand some."

The major smiled. "You understand much. I can see you have smart eyes, and a pretty face. You make a good spy."

"I'm not a spy. I'm a reporter. Working on a story for a wire service."

"An American wire service, yes? You are on the American side in the war?"

"I'm on nobody's side. It's my job to write about the war."

"But who pays you? The Americans—yes?"

Kate sized him up as he puffed on his Gitane. The major reminded her of a character in an old black-and-white World War II movie—the evil Japanese commander.

"I'm paid to write fairly about both sides. I try to tell the truth. They pay me to be impartial."

"Yes, yes. What are you doing here, in this area—so far from civilization? What are you writing about?"

"Corruption."

"This is news? The Americans pay you to write about this?"

"I'm paid by my wire service—they're a private company. The company pays me to write the truth!"

The major grew angry. "The truth about what? What about the camera? What have you photographed?"

"The cinnamon plantation."

"Cinnamon! What does cinnamon have to do with war?"

"I don't know. I'm trying to find out."

The major threw down an exposed roll of film he'd been holding. "I can't stand your smell, Miss White," he said, disgusted. "You must bathe now—to keep your American skin so fragrant." He signaled the soldier standing by the door to lead her out.

"He will take you to the river."

"And you made me drink from the puddle!"

The major laughed. "It's not healthy to drink from your bathwater, reporter." As Kate reached the doorway the major finished, "When you come back you tell the truth. Right now you smell like a liar."

The soldier led Kate from the hut down a narrow path to the river. He walked around behind her and untied the rope around her wrists.

"*Coi ra,* American!" Kate obeyed, and pulled off her fatigue shirt. She unbuttoned her pants and let them slide down her legs. The soldier took a small hotel-sized bar of soap from his pocket and held it out in his palm. Kate took it, looking unsmiling and resolute into the soldier's eyes as she did. Stepping out of her pants, she walked down the bank into the river with only her panties on. She stepped into the swollen river, feeling its soft muddy bottom under her feet, the slimy goo slipping between her toes.

Kate reveled in the feel of the soft river water on her body. But at the same time, thoughts of escape raced through her mind. If she made a go for it, she would be leaving Randy behind, but at least she would be able to seek help and come back for him. She looked out at the swift-moving current. It had been raining for weeks and the river had flooded over its banks—it would be a dangerous swim, even going downstream. She could be swept under. She tried to guess the speed of the current a few meters farther out from where she stood in a small protected cove. What she would need to do the moment the guard looked away was to hide under the muddy brown water. The swollen river was so thick with mud that the soldier wouldn't be able to see her even at close range. She would glide out underwater into the fast-moving current and be swept away. For as long as she could hold her breath she'd be hidden.

She was up to her knees in the water. She knew she needed to go deeper without causing suspicion. She inched farther into the river, bending forward as she went, rubbing the bar of soap down her legs. When the water covered her up to her waist, she removed her panties, scrubbing them with the bar of soap, offering a smile to the young man as she did. His cold Vietnamese stare remained frozen in place. She dipped down to her neck, stepping into her panties underwater. Testing the guard again, she dipped her head forward to wet her hair. Then she stood up straight to lather her hair with the soap. She decided, as she rubbed the soap in with her fingertips, that she would take a slow deep breath, then, bending to rinse her head, she would dive beneath the surface and make her escape. She felt her heart pounding as she counted down and prepared to dive.

6

Suddenly the sound of a helicopter echoed off the surface of the water from upriver. The major yelled a loud sharp command from the doorway of the hut, *"Dung lai! Dung lai!"*

The soldier rushed into the water and pulled Kate into the reeds by the riverbank. When the chopper appeared around the river bend, he ducked both himself and Kate beneath the water. After the chopper had safely passed, the major appeared at the river's edge. As the soldier pulled Kate's head above the surface, the major laughed, "Catch American fish!" He turned and headed back to the hootch as the soldier lead Kate out of the water. *"Mac vao!"* He ordered nastily, "Get dressed! Quickly, quickly!"

As Kate sat down again in front of the major, he lit a Gitane for her. "You feel better, Miss White?" He smiled as sweetly as he could.

"I'd feel better if I were back in Saigon—in a hot bath."

"Which brings me to my point. What were you doing out here in the jungle in the first place?"

"But I told you," she said. "The story is the same even after my bath."

"But you see," the major continued, keeping the fake smile on his face, "before or after your bath, I do not believe you."

"Why do you find it so hard to believe that I'm working on a story?"

"Precisely because there is nothing here of any interest to write about."

"I told you, the cinnamon."

"Cinnamon is precisely what I don't believe! What is the value of cinnamon these days? Who would be fools enough to harvest tree bark in the middle of our War of Liberation?" he guffawed and reached for his pack of Gitanes. "How could I believe such a thing?"

"Whether you believe it or not, that's the story."

"So where are your notes, Kate White? My men found no notes. Yet you say you're a writer?"

"My notebook was lost when we were trying to escape."

"If you have nothing to hide . . . then why were you trying to escape?"

"Your men, Major, were shooting at us!"

"Our soldiers saw you on the road . . . you and Randall Guest and the others. Everyone ran."

"Yes. You had killed the others."

"I have killed no one!"

"Your men . . ."

"It happens that if people are escaping, they are shot at. It's what you Americans do, yes?"

"I'm not American!"

"To me you are American. You work for them, you look like them, you smell like them!"

"The men you killed were Vietnamese . . ."

". . . who worked for Americans."

"They were my friends."

"Randall Guest is your officer?"

"He's my boss."

"Yes, your commander . . ."

Kate interrupted the major, greatly annoyed. "You don't believe anything I say! Why should I bother . . ."

". . . because I enjoy speaking with you. You should be happy to speak with someone who has an appreciation of you."

"I'm glad to know you appreciate me, Major, but I don't appreciate that your men killed my friends!"

"Who were these friends? Why do you travel with Vietnamese?"

"They were the film crew. They were with us to film the plantation."

"Yes, the plantation. And your job is to tell the truth and you talk of something so untruthful! My job is to get to the truth also . . . and I cannot believe your interest lies in cinnamon!"

The major stood abruptly, and paced slowly around Kate, looking down at her as he circled. He pulled a small, beat-up notebook from his breast pocket.

"You know how to lie—you're very good at it," said Kate. "You knew all along then, my story was about cinnamon. If you let me go," she looked up at him, "perhaps I'll be able to find the truth. Anyway, the Americans will come to find me, Major."

"I don't think they will be looking for you, Miss White—you are not reported as missing. You have been reported dead."

Hearing those words, Kate's heart sank. She tried hard not to show it.

"It seems by your notes you haven't learned much . . . or perhaps you're smart enough not to write everything down."

The major, listening to the sound of an approaching helicopter, walked to the door, and followed it with his eyes as it flew along the river. He turned back, walked over to a cupboard and pulled out a large bottle of French Vittel water.

He watched Kate's eyes closely as he poured her a tall glass of the water. "Perhaps this pure water will make you more truthful," he smiled, handing her the glass.

"You feel better now, Miss White? Now, perhaps you will answer me . . . what were you doing out here in the jungle?"

"But I told you, my story is still the same!"

"And I still do not believe you."

7

Peter and his best friend Marcus Zabriski sat side by side on the floor of a Huey UH1 helicopter as it snaked above the Song Tra Bong River west of Quang Ngai. Peter stared down intensely at the landscape below. Marcus read a Spider-Man comic.

For Peter it was easy to become lost within the beauty of the countryside. Looking down from the perch on the floor of the chopper, sitting beside the open door, the scenery below sometimes looked like a picture of the real thing, a copy, because it was so strikingly beautiful. Sometimes for Peter, lost in the psyche of war, it was difficult for him to tell the difference between what was real and what was not. They were flying a few thousand feet above the rice paddies, which was just high enough to create the illusion of unreality. Besides, the monsoon rain had turned the rice a green so bright it seemed to glow.

Together Peter and Marcus made a rather raggedy-looking team. Peter's straight brown hair had grown too long to meet army regulations, and Marcus could have been a poster of a California beach boy with his scraggly blond head of hair and mustache. If not for their uniforms and the weapons they carried, neither of them would have been suspected of being soldiers.

The two had been hooked up with a Vietnamese interpreter named Lan, who worked out of the main PIO office in Chu Lai. Lan was from an aristocratic Vietnamese family who had owned a rubber plantation, which they had sold to the French. He had been educated in a French school in Saigon and spoke English with a British accent. He was about the same height as Peter, six feet, which meant he was exceptionally tall for a Vietnamese. Peter had the feeling that Lan felt superior to the Americans he worked for. But as Marcus pointed out, he was not above taking their money. He was paid fifty dollars per day, a handsome wage for any Vietnamese.

Colonel Jake Broward waited in a clearing at the edge of Camp Fort Lauderdale, a large American detainee camp near Quang Ngai that held more than three thousand South Vietnamese. "Misplaced indigenous people" is the way the army put it. The truth was, though, the people were victims of Operation Broward County, during which soldiers had burned hundreds of small villages on the Batangan Penninsula. Peter and Marcus, army combat correspondents, were flying out to do a story on a prisoner—a young North Vietnamese who had surrendered—sick with malaria.

Broward was a stocky brute who kept a ramrod-stiff military bearing and had the close-cropped haircut to match. He was one of those lifers who looked as if he had been born with his combat boots on. He and his group of aides surrounded a young North Vietnamese prisoner who lay on his side on the ground, obviously too weak to stand. He was sweating profusely, suffering the chills of malaria.

The colonel cocked his head at the sound of the approaching chopper. A soldier ran to the center of the clearing, pulling the pin on a smoke grenade as he ran. He flung it to the far side of the clearing, upwind, where it burst into a Day-Glo green smoke cloud marking the spot for the chopper to land. The Huey came in quickly, flattening the smoke with its prop wash. As soon as the skids hit the ground, Peter and Marcus jumped off with their interpreter, Lan, following just behind.

Broward's chief flunky, a Lieutenant Zippo, greeted them. Zippo, tall and lanky, seemed as though he might've been created by a cartoonist with a sense of humor. The prop wash blew the bush hat off his small head. Marcus managed to catch it in midair and hand it back to him.

"Welcome to Fort Lauderdale, gentlemen," Zippo yelled above the engine noise, his beady blue eyes making an idiotic first impression. "Colonel Broward wants some snapshots of himself with the prisoner before your interrogation."

"We're here to get the prisoner's story," Peter informed the lieutenant.

Peter and Marcus approached the colonel, exchanging salutes while two of the colonel's men in the background tried unsuccessfully to stand the young NVA prisoner on his feet.

"Sir, I'm Sergeant Hill. This is Sergeant Zabriski . . . and our interpreter, Lan. We're here to get the prisoner's story . . ."

Everyone watched the North Vietnamese fall to the ground the moment Broward's men let go of his arms.

"Colonel, he's sick!" Peter said, seeing the man double up on the ground.

Lan spoke to the boy in a North Vietnamese dialect. "He says he has had chills for four days."

"Are you a doctor, son?" Broward argued.

"Sir, this boy should be in the hospital." Marcus bent down to feel the young man's forehead.

"Don't mess with my NVA, Sergeant," the colonel threatened. "Nothing wrong with my prisoner . . . ahh, Zablinski . . ."

"That's Zabriski, sir. Nothing wrong except he's about to die!"

Broward's callousness astonished them all. "This is inhumane treatment of a prisoner, sir," said Peter. "We've got to get him to Chu Lai."

Broward ordered, "Not until you take my photograph with him, Sergeant. You are standing on my ground, Hill. Part of Operation Broward County. That's an order, Sergeant! Take my picture with my prisoner, goddamnit!" Broward grabbed for Peter's camera.

Peter stepped back. "Colonel Broward, my job is to report stories for the army. I'm not to here to take a snapshot for your photo album!"

Broward screamed, "Zippo, *you* take the picture . . . get his camera!"

Marcus pushed Lieutenant Zippo aside before he could grab his Pentax. Zippo tripped over his own feet and fell. Peter and Marcus seized the
moment to lift the young NVA off the ground and rush him to the waiting chopper before Broward could stop them. Colonel Broward shot his
.45 pistol into the air. "Let my prisoner go or I'll have you court-martialed! Stop those men!" he yelled as the chopper lifted off the ground.
A couple of the colonel's aides hung on to the skids thinking they could
hold the chopper down. Broward continued to shoot wildly into the air.
"I'll get you! You'll see!" he shouted until he was out of rounds. As the
chopper continued to gain altitude, the colonel's men, one by one, let go
of the skids.

The chopper dipped its nose and began to gain speed. From the air, Peter
watched the colonel reload and take aim. He saw the small white cartoon
puffs of smoke appear at the end of the barrel of his .45. The colonel
looked like some sort of evil villain in a comedy. He continued to shout
obscenities even with the sound of his voice lost in the roar of the engine. All that was missing, Peter thought, were the cartoon balloons with
dialogue coming from his mouth.

"He's dangerous!" Peter yelled above the engine noise.

"He's like *Venom!*" Marcus held up his Spider-Man comic showing
Peter the villain.

8

Kate and Randy Guest were being interrogated together in the major's hut when the sounds of the Huey echoed from upriver. Kate's gaze met Randy's for a split second before she shifted her eyes toward the door. Knowing the chopper was returning from where it had headed upstream, Kate was determined not to miss this chance for escape. She jumped up and bolted toward the door. Randy, slow in getting up from the floor, was tackled by the lanky NVA blocking the doorway. Kate ran past and headed straight for the riverbank. She arrived panting and out of breath, just as the chopper carrying Peter and Marcus flew upriver.

From the air Peter saw a western woman dressed in army fatigues running along a trail toward the river—a Caucasian woman being chased by a North Vietnamese soldier. It was such an odd scene that he almost doubted what he saw. But he signaled the pilot, who circled the chopper back. They saw the woman running back up the path to a clearing in what appeared to be a small ville. The door gunner beside Peter sent a spray of bullets from his M-60 machine gun just over the woman's head at the NVA soldiers who suddenly appeared from the surrounding trees. Thinking she was being fired at, Kate dived to the ground, landing face-down in a puddle.

The chopper grazed the treetops as it roared into the clearing. The pilot flared out above the woman as the gunners on both sides sprayed the camp in all directions. Peter jumped down, landing in the puddle beside the woman. She turned her head toward him, her face just inches away from his, and smiled like a little girl. Peter grabbed her by the back of the shirt and before she was even on her feet had dragged her to the chopper. As the Huey started forward across the clearing, Kate grabbed the pilot's arm. "My partner's in there!" she screamed, pointing at the small hootch on one side of the clearing.

The pilot, without hesitating, spun the bird around again into the middle of the clearing. Marcus jumped off while the chopper was still moving and ran toward the small building. The door gunners fired from both sides. Seconds later, Marcus emerged with Randy. As a kind of coup de grâce, Marcus pulled a grenade off his belt and flung it back through the open doorway. The hootch exploded just as they reached the chopper. As the Huey lurched into the sky, shards of bamboo ricocheted off the blades. Peter reached out his hand to pull Marcus aboard. Kate smiled widely when she saw her battered Nikon hanging around his neck.

9

A spit-shined but rain-soaked line of troops stood at attention behind a low, freshly painted white picket fence on a well-kept lawn in front of Major General Cyrus Morgan's hootch. The scene reminded Peter of the tiny town of New Hampton, New Hampshire, where he had gone to prep school. The scene could've been in New England if it weren't for the temperature and the steady monsoon rain. Small, freshly painted houses replete with white-clapboard siding and shingle roofs were lined up along a paved road with their backyards perfectly aimed to offer the occupants an unobstructed view of the South China Sea. But in the front where the procession was held, it was definitely a re-creation of a suburban street in America. The general himself, a square, strongly built man with a head of luminescent silver hair and a deep tan, seemed oblivious to the rain that had soaked all the way through his fatigues. A small brass band wearing ponchos played a soggy, off-key rendition of "Singin' in the Rain" as General Morgan moved swiftly and quietly along the line of soldiers.

Peter and Marcus were the last two in the line. Colonel Broward followed a step behind the general, watching him pin a Bronze Star on each man's pocket flap. When the two of them reached Peter and Marcus, the colonel made a point of congratulating them personally, loud enough for the general to hear. "I'm especially proud that you both accomplished your mission. I expected nothing less from you two men. You followed my orders to the letter." Broward smiled ominously. "Both of you are deserving of far more than these small tokens on your chests." He paused, savoring a particularly evil smile and adding under his breath, "I'll make certain you get your just desserts, gentlemen."

Kate White, almost totally hidden beneath a rubber army poncho, stood across the road photographing the event with her battered Nikon F. After the ceremony ended she greeted Peter and Marcus with a warm, rain-drenched smile.

"What can I say to the two guys who saved my life?"

"I could think of some stuff," Marcus joked.

"You don't need to thank us—Colonel Broward did," Peter said. "That's enough for me."

"I'd like to buy you lunch at the Officers' Club," said Kate.

"No soup, please." Marcus joked, "Nothing with water in it." Marcus was happy—he was flying to Bangkok for R&R the next morning.

"They don't let lowlifes like us in," Peter warned her.

"You're with me." Kate smiled sweetly. "Whatever that means."

10

The Americal Division Officers' Club was nothing more than a thatch-roofed hut with a bamboo bar and a million-dollar view. Balanced precariously on the edge of a cliff above the turquoise South China Sea were about twenty round tables covered with starched white tablecloths—the tables along the ocean reserved for the ranking officers. The luminous phosphorescent color of the sea, visible from all four sides, gave the place the quality and feel of a movie set. It was as if one of the grand old Hollywood moguls had pointed to the spot and decreed, "Build it there." The club was, in its own way, a powerful place. Many of the life-and-death decisions of warfare in Quang Ngai Province were made over drinks around the cloth-covered tables. General Morgan, as division commander, garnered the table with the best view, the one that sat most precipitously above the sea. Over the edge is right where the general liked to be.

General Cyrus Morgan sat with Colonel Jake Broward and Major General Nguyen Tao, a slight, nattily dressed man, commander of the Seventeenth ARVN Division. It was too early for lunch. Except for their aides who sat at an adjoining table, the club was empty. Kate, Peter, and Marcus took a table at the opposite corner of the room next to the bar. A pretty Vietnamese waitress, dressed in traditional black pajamas and conical hat, brought them drinks. Peter and Marcus drank Seagrams with 7-Up. Kate had a vodka and tonic.

"I've heard a lot about you guys since yesterday. I've been doing some investigative reporting." She smiled.

"All lies, I'm sure," Marcus said, sucking down his whiskey in a matter of seconds. "You gotta talk to the horse's mouth to get the real shit."

"Forgive Marcus's manners," Peter said, "He grew up in the slums of Saigon."

"You were roommates at Yale?"

"For six months—until we joined up."

"That's a long leap—Yale to Vietnam."

"Never would've guessed how long," said Peter.

Marcus swallowed. "You doing a story?" he asked Kate, "I mean, about us?"

"Is there one?" Kate raised her brown eyebrows.

"We were onto something when we spotted you," Peter told her.

"Yeah, but he died." Marcus frowned.

Peter continued, "We were out on a story. At Broward's camp, Fort Lauderdale, down by Quang Ngai. Broward's men had captured a North Vietnamese prisoner who was ready to talk about his unit."

Marcus cut in, "He was the body in the chopper when we picked you up."

Kate's eyes lit up. "Did he say anything? Anything at all?"

"His unit was supposed to capture a plantation of some sort," Peter told her. "That's all we got from him."

Kate looked disappointed. "That's it?"

"He said Broward's troops knew about their operation—they'd been tipped off somehow. His unit had been ambushed by Broward's men."

"A cinnamon plantation?" Kate asked.

"Spice." Marcus smiled. "Can you beat that?" Suddenly his look turned sour when Lieutenant Zippo marched up their table packing his shit-eating grin along with him. They cut their conversation short for the lieutenant's arrival.

"Thanks for the warm welcome," he said. "Sorry I can't repay you boys in kind, but you are definitely off limits in my club." Still smiling, he ordered, "Have one for the road, then get the fuck out."

Zippo turned to Kate. "Excuse my language, Miss White—General Morgan and Colonel Broward request the pleasure of your company at their table. The general's guest is General Tao."

Kate looked toward the general's table. The three officers looked back eagerly, smiling when they caught her glance. "Yes, I see," Kate said to Zippo. "I'll join them on one condition, that Sergeants Hill and Zabriski are allowed to stay and drink at your bar—in your club, as you call it."

Zippo looked puzzled—seemingly an expression not unusual for him. "Mmmmh, well . . ."

"On your tab, Lieutenant?"

"That's bribery, Miss White."

"Something I'm sure you know all about." Kate stood as the lieutenant pulled her chair out for her. "You know . . . not only are you an asshole, Lieutenant, you're a righteous one."

"Appreciate the constructive criticism, ma'am." Zippo smiled.

"I'll join you guys for a drink in a few," Kate said as she pushed her chair out. "I have some unfinished business with Colonel Broward . . . and his friends."

The two generals and Colonel Broward stood up starch-straight as Kate approached their table. They were all smiles. After all, she was a beautiful woman. Each of the three men seemed to inspect her closely as she shook their hands. Since he knew her, Jake Broward did the introductions. "General Morgan, General Tao—meet Kate White." Peter caught sight of Broward's hand swiping Kate on the ass. He saw her let it go.

"An unexpected pleasure. Your reputation precedes you." General Morgan flashed his heavy smile.

"That's not good. You'll have your guard up," she said.

"Miss White, my guard is always up."

"General Tao, let me introduce Kate White, the much-respected United Press International correspondent."

"Quite an honor, Miss White."

"Yes, I've heard you're an honorable man, General." She smiled as she shook his hand.

"In the end, honor is all a man has." General Tao looked up into her eyes.

"Or a woman," Kate continued.

"Perhaps even more so."

"Perhaps equally so," Kate smiled.

"A woman's honor must be more of a personal thing—isn't it so? While a man's honor is mostly a matter of tradition."

"I'm not an expert on men."

"But here you are in the middle of a man's world."

"If you refer to the war, I agree. But your country is a matriarchal society—is it not, General?"

General Tao was surprised at the brashness of this woman he'd only just been introduced to. "*Matriarch* is mostly an honorable title given the eldest woman in the family."

"There's that word *honor* again. To be honest, General, I don't find much honor in your country. Except, of course, of money." She sat down in the chair Colonel Broward offered.

Broward cut her off. "Reporters find it easy to insult even the highest ranks."

"Especially the highest ranks," laughed Morgan. "What are you drinking, Miss White?"

"Vodka and tonic, thank you." Kate quickly shifted to business. "As long as I'm in your company, General Morgan, would you answer a few questions about Operation Broward County? There's talk about a missing company . . . one of the colonel's units."

Morgan threw a quick glance at Broward.

"You were invited to drink with us, Miss White." Morgan looked annoyed. "Not to interrogate."

"To honor then." Kate lifted her glass as soon as the waiter put it down. Realizing she was going to get nowhere with the three tight-lipped officers, she stood abruptly and said with a cryptic smile, "It's been a pleasure, gentlemen . . ."

"Pleasure is something we all know about—men and women, equally," said General Tao, hastily pushing his chair back as he stood up.

"Equally," Kate smiled over her shoulder as she headed back to her table.

The three officers were left standing in their stiff officer's fatigues with angry looks on their faces. As she crossed the room, Kate heard the word *bitch* spoken quietly but angrily, through the colonel's tightly clenched teeth. Peter turned around in his seat when he heard Kate approach. He caught Broward looking across at them. It was just a quick impression, but Peter again saw the evil in the man's eyes.

Joined by Kate, Peter and Marcus continued to joke about Marcus's prospects for getting stoned, getting laid, and getting the clap on R&R. They agreed on 100 percent for all three. Though Kate was happy to be back with the boys, she was, as usual, all business, "I want to get out to the A Shau Valley tomorrow. Can you guys help me?"

"Not me, ma'am," Marcus answered, swiveling around on his bar stool. "I'm on the R&R bird to Bangkok at oh eight hundred tomorrow. Heaven on wheels!" He circled his eyeballs to signify the good time he was expecting.

Peter turned to Kate, "I'll take you. If you don't mind a stop at my LZ on the way. I've got a jeep to return."

"Can you put me up for the night?" Kate asked, causing Marcus's eyebrows to raise a notch.

"It can be arranged," Peter replied.

"Good," said Kate, in a businesslike voice, "but first I need to use the correspondents' phone to call my bureau."

"I'll walk you to the PIO," Peter said, feeling like an actor as he spun theatrically off his barstool at the same time as he downed the last of his drink. He gave Marcus a warm bear hug. It was obvious to Kate that their connection went deep.

"'Bye for now, Pete ol' buddy," Marcus laughed. "See you in a week. If I can still walk." Marcus had a way of always seeming light. It's what made most people think of him as "that surfer dude" or at least, unmistakably, a Californian. But Peter knew him better than anyone—he knew that Marcus's breezy attitude was just a cover. Just like his humor was. A few millimeters below the surface, there was a deep sadness.

"The war will be waiting for you. So will I," Peter told his friend.

Marcus truly appreciated it when Kate gave him a warm hug. "Why don't you stay and get a start on your R&R right here?" she suggested. "On Lieutenant Zippo's tab!"

"Not a bad idea." Marcus laughed, swiveling around to face the Vietnamese bartender. "Another Seven and Seven, dear."

Peter offered his friend a toast: "Keep yer head down, ol' buddy . . . and yer pecker up."

As Peter and Kate walked up to the door, the wind blew a fine spray of rain through the screen and across their faces. Kate lifted her poncho over both their heads as they walked out into the steamy monsoon rain heading for the division PIO office. They found themselves close together for the first time under the small, contained space of the poncho. The humidity captured beneath the rubberized fabric made the air stifling. Peter realized that although Kate was half a head shorter than he was, they walked with the same gait. He put his arm around her waist to hold her close enough to keep her dry. He felt the tight muscles in her lower back. Also, he felt a subtle release of tension, which told him she trusted his touch. Beginning to let her guard down, Kate welcomed his hand, feeling protected by it. Peter lifted the poncho to steal a look at this woman whom he had begun to feel was quite remarkable. Her eyes were focused straight ahead giving him a chance to study the delicate profile of her face in the dim light beneath the poncho. It surprised him how much softer she looked from the side. Kate felt his gaze and turned to look up at him. Then he saw how bright and piercing her green eyes were—bright like the green of the jungle during a rain. Peter saw something else as well—a definite sadness in her eyes, as if something was buried behind them.

The dull thud of an artillery shell exploded somewhere over the mountains to the west—near LZ Danger, where they were headed. His thoughts quickly pulled him back into the world of reality, where the two of them walked—the Americal Division Headquarters, Chu Lai, Vietnam, 1968. They both knew that there, you didn't allow yourself to slide into reverie for too long. Doing that got you killed, goddamnit.

In the PIO hootch a small, private area had been sectioned off with sheets of unpainted plywood where correspondents could write their stories, then phone them in to their bureaus. The walls were covered with hastily penciled phone numbers and all sorts of writer's graffiti about the war. The room was empty. Kate went straight to the phone and was lucky to get through to UPI in Saigon directly, without a hitch. She asked for Randy Guest. Peter stood beside her and as she spoke on the phone he read the names of cities someone had drawn in red ink on a crude map of South Vietnam. His eyes followed the map north, then traveled west from Chu Lai through Tam Ky, Mang Son, Ta Rau, Mang Ca, to the A Shau Valley . . .

"Hello, I'm fine," she said, her voice suddenly becoming excited. "Had a drink with General Morgan and General Tao and Jake Broward, if you can believe that! Yes, all at the same table." She paused to listen to the voice on the phone. Then she said, "Nothing, nada, not a bloody thing. But they're up to something big. I'm sure of it. All my doubt is gone. It was written in mashed potatoes all over their faces." While Kate listened to Randy on the line, she began, distractedly, to look at Peter as if she was assessing the young soldier she remembered she was with. "No, no, I'm all right. I'm in good hands." She smiled up at him and as she did, she reached for his hand, getting his forearm instead. She continued, somewhat awkwardly at first, to hold on anyway. "Sergeant Hill is escorting me out to the A Shau Valley tomorrow." She continued, absentmindedly running a finger along his arm. "Yes, he's the one who just happened over our little prison camp. Don't worry, I'll find a cot for the night. Yes, I'll ring . . . the second we're back." Peter felt an unexpected thrill as Kate's hand moved from his arm to the front of his shirt where she began to steer her fingertips between two of his buttons. Realizing how close they were, Peter felt that the humid monsoon air somehow defined the space between them. He was drawn closer to her, feeling he was pushing the warm air out of the way until suddenly there was no space between them at all. His chest touched hers—her hand trapped between them. She pulled it out. As she spoke into the phone he could feel her breath on his neck. "Yes, a nice long rest." She continued speaking without really knowing what she was saying. To Peter her words had become just sound. "Bangkok sounds wonderful," she said to the invisible man on the other end. Those huge green eyes lifted up and pierced right through Peter's brain. "Yes, I will. No, I don't think he'll mind." Peter placed his hand gently against the back of her head, feeling her hair, short and soft and completely wonderful. He listened to her say, "Yes, me too," then she hung up the phone. She spoke slowly with her lips just inches from his. "Randy says I'm to give you a big hug from both of us." She moved closer and even before she had finished speaking, their lips touched. He felt her hand on his back, up inside his shirt, her soft palm asking questions of him. She needed to back away, to think, but Peter didn't let her. Instead, with his arm still around her back, he pulled her hard against him. Then he felt Kate soften, her body falling into his. He felt the surrender. He pressed his chest against her breasts. For a brief moment they stopped to breathe, to look into each other's eyes until they were drawn together again. They kissed, seeking out, as if on a map, the direction they both wanted to travel.

11

Monsoon season in Vietnam meant almost constant rain. It meant that the sky, which was usually a magnificent light blue punctuated with puffed-up white clouds, turned into an ominous steel-gray color upon which clouds were painted black. On the ground, the fine dusty earth, usually rock hard, became a soft mushy substance that swallowed almost everything that tried to move across it. It was as if the entire country turned into quicksand. Whenever the rain stopped for a short time, it was doing so only to give false hope, promising that things would dry out. When it would start again it seemed to fall with even greater ferocity than it had before. It rained so hard at times it felt almost like being beneath the ocean.

When Peter and Kate drove out of the gate of American headquarters in Chu Lai and headed south on Highway One, the rain started again. The section of the highway they traversed was made of dirt already turned to mud. The ruts dug by the big two-and-a-half-ton trucks didn't fit the small wheels of the jeep. The trip, especially since the sky had suddenly turned a bluish black, was precarious from the start. There was no guarantee at all that they would make it to their destination eight kilometers to the south and west. But there was simply no other choice available. Choppers didn't fly in the kind of weather they were facing—especially not at night in a blue-black sky.

Peter fought to keep the jeep on the washed-out stretch of road, the link between Chu Lai and the lonely outpost, Landing Zone Danger, which he called home. Only a few minutes out from Chu Lai the rain fell faster, pelting the jeep so hard it sounded like someone was punching on the canvas top just inches above their heads. A light spray of rain came through the canvas anyway—and there were a few steady streams where the top was torn. The small wipers couldn't keep up with the volume that fell against the windshield. After a few kilometers all the light was gone. They could hardly see. Peter's goal was to keep the jeep from skidding into the deep drainage ditch on either side of the muddy road. And not to feel too afraid of the five or so kilometers of road that lay ahead. Then came sniper shots from somewhere off to the right. They heard the ping of a bullet on the sheet metal of the jeep.

"Fuck!" Peter turned the headlights off then leaned forward with his face almost up against the windshield trying desperately to see the road. "How the fuck can he see us in this fucking rain?"

"Should I shoot?" Kate asked, tensely. Without waiting for an answer, she grabbed Peter's M-16 from between the front seats, expertly shoved in a magazine, and pointed the barrel out the open side of the jeep into the blackness of the storm. She selected automatic with her thumb, pulled the trigger, and sprayed ten rounds into the dark.

"Fuck!" they yelled in unison when the sniper instantly returned fire.

A moment later the firing stopped and everything was quiet save for the rain and some mortar tubes popping off illumination rounds over LZ Danger, still three or four kilometers away from them in the darkness. The two of them remained hypervigilant, aware of every sound, no matter how small—any change in the engine tone, the sound of the rain, their own breathing. Sounds became amplified in weird ways. The normal engine whine could sometimes sound like a scream. A burst of rain against the windshield became the sound of bullets shattering glass. They were lost in a state of knowing that someone was seeking them out in the dark, trying to put a bullet in their brains. Their minds and bodies were completely tense, all emotions shut down, buried. Peter, somehow—he didn't know how—was able to follow the muddy dirt road in the pitch black, in the rain without the headlights on. Essentially, he remained on the road without being able to see it. Peter had noticed before that impossible things became possible in situations like the one they were in. Also, if they survived, it would seem as though they'd lived a lifetime together. War operated on a different sense of time. War was different. And the people who went through it were made different because of it.

In the sky above the hill that LZ Danger sat on, the illumination rounds drifted down quickly with the weight of the rain pushing on the small parachutes they dangled from. The LZ appeared in the prism of the rain on the windshield like a painting by El Greco with the black sky transformed into gold and silver. The light glowed and drifted as the parachutes were blown sideways by the storm. The sight was beyond eerie. It reached the level of art. An art critic would've called it magnificent.

For the remainder of the journey, neither of them spoke a word. They never abandoned, for an instant, the state of awareness that would get them there alive.

Kate, who sat sideways in her seat, her back to Peter, was completely focused on the cold, wet metal under her fingertip—the trigger of the M-16. The light from the illumination rounds showed the ruts in the road just enough to allow Peter to speed up. Peter drove, at the same time lost in the beauty of the El Greco in the windshield.

12

It was midnight when the jeep sloshed to a halt in the mud beside the heavily sandbagged guard post where the road finally met the perimeter of LZ Danger. Peter knew the guards would be wary of the jeep arriving in the rain with its headlights off at that hour of night. He knew too that they would have to determine if the jeep was friendly or filled with Vietcong dressed as Americans. As he pulled up he watched a soldier in the guard tower focusing a night vision scope on them. Peter could see a tiny speck of light reflected off the lens as the guard followed their movement. As they pulled up to the gate, Peter knew that he and Kate were probably in the sights of at least twenty weapons, including the four 50-caliber machine guns mounted on the back of a two-and-a-half-ton truck.

When Peter stopped the jeep, the MP on duty warily stepped out of the sandbagged guard post, his .45 pointed directly at Peter's temple. As he leaned down for a closer look under the jeep's canvas top, a river of water ran off the hood of his poncho directly onto the floor of the jeep. It baffled the guard that anyone would be on the road at that late hour, especially in this weather, especially with a woman. When he was close enough, the guard recognized Peter. He focused the beam of his flashlight on Kate's face.

"She's a UPI reporter—I'm taking her out to the A Shau Valley to-morrow," Peter said before the guard had the chance to ask.

"Oh" is all the guard said. The A Shau had an ominous reputation. Everyone, even those who hadn't been there, had heard stories. And those who had been—those who told the stories—were happy to have gotten out alive. Nobody ever wanted to go back. The men who had stayed for a month or more and lived to tell came back changed.

The guard, still perplexed but finding no reason to hold them any longer, pushed open the gate waving them through.

The PIO office was nothing more than a rickety one-room tin-and-plywood shack with two wooden steps leading up to a screen door. When Peter wasn't in the field, this was where he typed out his stories before he radioed them in to Chu Lai. This was also where he slept on a solitary cot in the back of the hootch.

Exhausted and soaked through to the bone, the two of them pushed through the doorway into the conspicuously empty room, feeling like the journey of only eight kilometers had taken a lifetime. Though it was dark, or maybe *because* it was, it felt safe—a place not to be seen, to hide. Although a fine mist blew through the screens along the wall, the room was relatively dry. Peter felt around in the dark for the tin of matches he kept on his small working table and lit the utility candle beside his typewriter.

He spoke nervously, acutely aware he was alone in the room with Kate. "Let me find us some dry fatigues," he offered, walking to the back where he opened the footlocker beside his cot. "Sorry, only one pair. They're damp."

"Damp beats soaked. We can share them," said Kate. "I guess you get to wear the pants."

Peter handed her the shirt. "Sorry there's no privacy in here."

"Why should I mind?" She immediately began peeling off her wet clothes without even bothering to turn her back. "I'm in the presence of friends, I presume."

"I haven't seen a woman naked in quite a while—up close, that is . . . well, not a woman . . ."

". . . a *white* woman," Kate said.

". . . yes, for quite a while."

Peter took off his wet fatigues and pulled on the dry pair of pants.

He couldn't take his eyes off Kate. From the side, he watched her fingers as she unbuttoned her shirt. She did it slowly, distractedly; her thoughts were somewhere else. She was squinting to read the big map of I Corps Peter had thumbtacked on the wall, her eyes following the line of red tacks he had stuck on certain villages nearby: Than Tra, Tri Binh, My Lai, An Lay. A line of red dots led from the coast above Quang Ngai along the Song Tra Bong River heading upstream into the highlands.

"Stories?" asked Kate.

"You guessed."

Kate's eye fell on a green-colored one that was north of Chu Lai and inland from Tam Ky. "What's that?" she asked, pushing her shirt back on her shoulders until it slid down her back onto the floor.

"A Buddhist temple I came upon," Peter said, catching his breath. "It's very peaceful. When you're inside it's like the war doesn't exist."

"Have you written about it?" Kate stopped what she was doing to look at him.

He looked at the green tack, perplexed. "I'd never thought of it as a story."

"Sounds like it would make a beautiful one."

"Like I said. It's like an oasis in the middle of the war."

"That could be the story." She smiled.

His eyes drifted back. He wasn't able to keep his eyes off Kate's body. He felt like he was twelve years old again, sneaking a look at a woman's breasts. He was overwhelmed by Kate's raw beauty and at her shameless nakedness. He wasn't yet prepared to accept that he was about to taste Kate's flesh. He, alone in the world, was in this tiny shack on a mountaintop in Vietnam with this beautiful woman.

She began to unbutton the fly of her wet fatigue pants.

"I'll take you to the temple," he told her.

"Please show it to me."

With her thumbs tucked into the waist, she pushed down her pants together with her panties, which were soaked as well. All the while Peter stood still marveling at her fluid motion feeling like an artist would, studying the movements of a model he was about to paint. As she bent forward to push her pants down over her knees, her breasts lit by the candlelight became fuller and even more beautiful. Her movements made the flame flicker, which in turn created dancing patterns across her body.

"It feels so good to be out of those wet clothes," she said stepping away from the pile on the floor. Stretching out her strong, thin frame, she leaned her head far back, lifting her arms like a dancer above her head. Peter tried not to stare.

"Can I make us some tea?" she asked.

"Coffee's all we've got. I'll put a heat tab on the stove."

Peter handed her the clean fatigue shirt.

"No, let me." She pushed her arms through the sleeves of the fatigue shirt, not bothering to button it up. Then she brought the candle from the table and kneeled down on the floor with it so she could see what she was doing. She took the heat tab from Peter and set it on top of the stove, lighting it with the candle.

Without looking up at him, she said, "Peter, I will sleep with you if you like. I'm saying this because we're alone in this hootch in the middle of nowhere—and it's bloody cold. And the two of us, in case either of us was about to forget, are in the middle of an insane war."

"Don't do it because you feel you owe me."

"It's because I want to." She spoke with her back still to him. "If you want to know the truth, I've wanted to ever since you pulled me from that puddle."

Peter was speechless. He felt like he had fallen into some sort of unreal dream. He'd been in-country for nearly six months and the only Western women he had seen were the Donut Dollies who'd flown out to the LZ a few times and served them hot dogs on a grill.

He unfolded a quilted poncho liner and set it on the floor for Kate to sit on. Then he went to fill his aluminum canteen cup from the jerry can beside the cot by the back door. Instead of using the water from the can he held the cup outside the back door, filling it with runoff from the roof. He returned and handed Kate the full cup. She sat down cross-legged on the poncho liner stirring in a packet of C ration coffee with her finger. He sat down awkwardly beside her. When the coffee was hot they took turns drinking from the cup listening to the heavy monsoon rain beat loudly against the corrugated metal roof, punctuated now and then by the thudding of 50-caliber machine guns from the perimeter.

While they were having coffee, Peter lit up a Camel for each of them.

"So—who are you, Peter?" she asked.

Peter wondered if that was her technique for an interview. Did she always begin with such a big question? He had to think for a minute before coming up with a smart answer. "That's a loaded question for a guy in a war."

"Everything's loaded in a war" was her comeback.

"And nothing's what it seems . . ."

"Or maybe everything"—she paused—"is just what it seems."

"Sounds like the mind of a reporter at work," Peter said. "Someone used to getting to the bottom of things."

"You could say so. But that doesn't necessarily mean I don't have a heart."

"Do you dare let it show?" He studied her closely as she stared into the candle flame.

She looked at him. "What do you think?"

Suddenly Peter was overcome with an intense longing. He reached over and undid a button on her fatigue shirt. "Let's see if there's a heart in there."

Kate put her hand over his, moving it onto her breast. "Can you feel something beating?"

"Yes." But what he felt even stronger was his own heart pounding in his chest. He leaned closer, kissing her on her lips.

She backed away. "I'd like to know something about you, first. Like why you're here. You could have stayed away. Gone to Canada, for instance."

"I wanted to see what was going on. I was in college for the wrong reason—to keep out of the draft. What it really came down to was fear. I was afraid. After I realized that, I knew I had to come."

"So you joined the army to prove something?"

Peter pushed open Kate's shirt. "Like that. I was feeling afraid to touch you—to move closer to where we might want to go. So I needed to prove to myself I could do it."

"You're a brave man."

"Not really—not after what you said."

"You mean, that I would sleep with you."

He smiled.

"I meant you were brave because you came to Vietnam."

"Oh . . ." He laughed. "I thought you meant . . ."

"I could've slapped your hand."

"I guess you could've."

"Perhaps I'm not ready."

"Maybe not."

"Maybe I am."

Kate leaned forward, crossing the space between them, placing her lips lightly against his.

"So, what have you proved by coming here?" She spoke with her mouth against his, her warm breath filling him with hope.

Peter laughed. "Nothing. I just showed up."

"I'm glad you did." Kate reached over and started to unbutton his fatigue pants.

"If I hadn't, I wouldn't have met you." He cupped his hand beneath her left breast.

"Do you have a political view?" Kate asked.

He leaned his head down. He kissed her breast. He felt her hard nipple brush against his cheek. "War sucks," he spoke into her breast as if it contained a microphone.

"You're evading the question."

"I'm being as truthful as I know how. The longer I'm here, the less I know what's up."

"That's the truth."

"I showed up real gung-ho. We both were, Marcus and I. But now . . . I really don't know."

Kate held his cheeks in her hands and kissed him hard this time. Peter felt her tongue searching for his.

She pulled back again. "Do you have more candles?"

Peter stood up and walked to the back of the hootch, returning with a full box of utility candles. "Let's light them all. In Australia the Aborigines perform a ceremony where they surround themselves with fire. It protects them."

Kate began placing the candles around them. "I've always had this fantasy about doing this," she said.

"Maybe we can stop the war for a while," Peter said, helping her until the circle was complete.

"Let's see if it works." She let her shirt slide off her shoulders onto the floor as she leaned toward him, pressing her mouth hard against his. A machine gun began firing on the perimeter.

Kate pulled back. "Ritual's not working yet."

Peter had a chance to look at Kate's beautiful face glowing in the soft light of the candles. She frowned. He reached up and wiped away the frown on her forehead with his thumb, then gently pulled her down onto the poncho liner. The machine gun fired off another burst.

"We have to try harder," Peter said.

She lifted her head up and kissed him. "I'll be out of a job if we end the war," Kate said.

"What would you do? Find another?" he asked.

"Write a book, probably. About this one."

"Will I be in it?"

"Have to wait and see."

Peter touched Kate's cheek, staring deep into her green eyes. The machine guns on the perimeter, after a few final bursts, finally fell silent. The rain continued to fall in torrents, the large drops pelting the metal roof like some primitive drumbeat. The wind gusted outside, sending waves of fine spray through the screens. Their bodies were coated with a delicate mist. The light from the windblown candles made their shadows dance on the walls of the hootch.

"Our ritual finally seems to be working," Kate said. They began to kiss with pent-up passion. They tasted the nervous sweat from the ride from Chu Lai on each other's skin. Then there were all the new smells and flavors to taste on bodies meeting for the first time. To Peter, Kate had the harsh flavor of Australia. He tasted to her like a young American—a teenager still. Kate wanted to—she tried to—lick him all over, not wanting to miss anything about him.

They relished the process of discovering each other's bodies. There was so much to know and so much that could be learned from the senses. It was as if they sought safety in each other—a place to escape to—if only for a short time. That was it! They wanted to escape into each other. There seemed to be two opposing forces at play, the desire to escape and the desire to come close. They melted the desires into one and the same thing. Yet they became consumed by the need to get to their final destination, urgently, before the machine guns began to fire and the war started up again.

Their lovemaking, heightened by the sound of the rain and the shadows dancing on the walls, was at once primitive and otherworldly. They both had a physical need to feel pain—as if they didn't deserve anything more than that.

And with the reality of war as a kind of glass shell around them, they caressed each other as if this were their only chance. Each kiss was loaded with a meaning all its own. No kiss was to be wasted. Each one became more precious than the last because they knew that as each kiss was used up, there were fewer left to give. Their minds struggled to keep up with the speed of their passion, asking questions of all the new sensations bombarding them.

Peter slid his mouth down Kate's neck, his tongue drinking in the fine dew on the surface of her skin. Kate pushed him away in order to pull the poncho liner out from under her back. Then she fell back hard against the floor as if she wanted to hurt herself. Pulling Peter down on top of her, she dug her nails into his back. He grabbed her arms, pinning them down and to the sides. Pressing them hard against the floor, he bent his head down to kiss her again. Kate grabbed the side of his mouth with her teeth, holding his cheek that way until she reached an orgasm. Then he lowered himself down against her stomach and breasts, pressing himself into her until he came.

They lay against one another for a long time, kissing gently, as if each of them was apologizing to the other for causing pain. Finally, they crawled around the circle of candles, blowing them out until the hootch fell dark. The ritual was complete.

Kate said, "For a few minutes I forgot where we were."

The muffled thud of a distant mortar blast reached the hootch. "Hear that? That's where you are—you are in the boonies with a GI who sleeps on a hard cot," Peter said. "Let's see if we can find the cot. It's not soft but it's dry."

"I don't like soft mattresses. I'll take a stiff cot any time." Kate chuckled.

An illumination round popped into the sky above the hootch, giving the room an eerie blue-white glow.

"Top or bottom?"

"I'm from *Down Under*."

"Oh yes, I almost forgot who I was with. The beautiful Australian woman reporter, isn't it? Why did you come out to this godforsaken place anyway?"

"I forget . . . to repay you for saving my life? Or maybe it was just because I wanted to make love with you. You're taking me out to the A Shau Valley in the morning, remember? You know they won't let us civilians out in the field alone."

"It's dangerous out here," Peter said.

"You're here to protect me."

"Who's going to protect me from you?"

"You'll have to fight that one for yourself."

Peter lifted Kate in his arms and carried her to the cot.

"A man with manners and tradition—I like that," she said as he set her down.

A mortar exploded outside, the flash lighting the hootch like a strobe light. Peter pulled Kate off the cot onto the floor. He ran for his M-16. Kate scrambled to find her shirt then searched for her camera bag. Another mortar exploded somewhere in the middle of the LZ. Peter pulled Kate toward the door knowing the hootch wasn't sandbagged.

"I need to find my camera!" she screamed.

"Forget it, Kate! We've got to get to a bunker!"

A mortar exploded twenty meters in front of them just as they headed out of the hootch. The blast shook the building, rattling the tin roof. They heard two more explosions on another part of the LZ. Then they ran for the bunker. Peter pulled Kate quickly to the closest bunker where they jumped down through the small opening into a pool of waist-deep water. The bunker was hot with the breath of soldiers standing shoulder to shoulder, their weapons already in position aimed out the small ports between the sandbags. Peter recognized Staff Sergeant Ed Ames, a LRRP with a reported forty-nine kills. He had a pile of magazines stacked up in front of him. Peter, embarrassed, asked him for ammo, having left his bandoleers in the hootch.

"Shoot with your typewriter, Hill." Ames smiled good-naturedly, his silver front tooth sparkling in the light of an artillery flare. He handed him a couple of magazines from his pile. Peter put his arm around Kate, who pressed against him shivering from the cold water. In the light of the flare outside, once again Peter studied Kate's face from the side.

"Guess you're caught with your pants down," he whispered in her ear.

"Story of my life," she whispered back.

13

The two of them sat close together five thousand feet in the air on the bench seat of a Huey while the pilot tried unsuccessfully to prod his way through the thickening curtain of clouds covering the route out to the A Shau Valley. As was often the case during monsoon season they would be forced to wait out the weather. The chopper settled down toward the ground in slow circles, all eyes watching as the thick carpet of gray-green jungle below came closer by the second. Miraculously, it seemed, a small clearing appeared in the middle of the sea of thick jungle that stretched for miles in every direction. Peter wondered how the pilot was able to find the place—how did he know it was there?

A shroud of fog hung protectively above the clearing. The place had a magical quality. The isolated silence became palpable after the engine was shut down and the heavy rotor blades lumbered in ever-slower rotations. With the blades making their final revolution, the solitude became complete—there simply was no sound at all. Everyone turned to look when the door gunner flicked open the top of his Zippo lighter. It seemed as loud as if the soldier had just let out a scream.

When the fog began to part, it was like a curtain opening on a stage. The fuselage of a huge downed cargo plane had been hidden at the far end of the clearing. A propeller plane from another war, its gi-

54

gantic wings poked through twenty years or more of twisted jungle growth.

Kate jumped down from the chopper with her camera in hand. Peter pulled his .45 from its holster following her cautiously toward the plane while the chopper crew watched curiously. As the two approached the plane they found themselves faced with dozens of smiling faces peering out of the leaves beneath the wings —faces instantly they recognized as Montagnards, primitive, friendly mountain people. Peter returned his gun to the holster, holding his hands up cowboy-style, above his head. One by one, the Montagnards stepped out from under the wings. The village men—all of them under five feet tall—came out first. Their hair was long and worn in braids. They wore nothing but loincloths on their dark bodies. The women and children, who were completely naked, followed. The group gathered around the two Westerners smiling, chattering among themselves. They were fascinated with Kate's camera. Neither Kate nor Peter understood the ancient Montagnard dialect so there were no words to bridge the gap between their cultures. Kate began to photograph them.

The villagers seemed most eager to show off their airplane. They tugged Kate and Peter through an opening in the vines. Inside the plane, in the center of the huge empty fuselage, a cooking fire burned, the smoke floating out through a hole cut in the ceiling. The village men squatted around the fire to finish the meal the intruders had interrupted. Kate and Peter were invited to sit and were offered plates of cooked insects. Peter politely picked up a grasshopper by the leg and ate it. Kate followed his lead. Though the Montagnards continued to talk among themselves, the Westerners remained silent, feeling privileged to be participants in this incredible scene. It was as if the strange airplane they sat in had flown them back twenty or thirty years in time and landed in the middle of the war France was fighting with Vietnam. Kate took pictures with the flash—which created a murmur among the people each time it went off. The soft cackling of the Montagnard voices, the acrid smell of the smoke—all of this created a surrealistic world until from outside, the whine of the Huey's jet engine firing up brought Peter and Kate back to reality. When they stood up to go, Peter took off his bush hat and placed it respectfully on the chief's head. Kate pulled a pair of sunglasses from her camera bag and handed them to the small man standing beside her. Everyone laughed when he tried them on.

The women and children were waiting outside as the group emerged from the plane. The entire village followed them to the chopper, waiting and watching as the strange mechanical bird lifted off the ground and headed into the sky. As the Huey gained altitude, one of the door gunners, seemingly crazed by the war—or perhaps just bored—opened fire with his M-60 machine gun, laughing madly as he saw the villagers scatter and run for cover. Peter kicked the barrel with his boot, knocking it skyward.

"What the fuck?" The gunner started to turn his gun toward Peter. He stopped when he saw the look in Peter's eyes. He was angry enough to kill, so the gunner backed off. Suddenly they were back to the war.

14

The Huey lumbered along in the moist air high above the lush rain-soaked jungle. The farther west they flew, the higher the mountaintops became until they seemed to summon them into what was then the most dangerous valley in all of Vietnam—the A Shau. The destination now in sight, the chopper pointed its nose down, starting its quick descent. LZ Strange, the westernmost command post for Operation Broward County, sat perched on top of a steep-sided mountain looming above the deep valley floor. It had been positioned tactically to cut the North Vietnamese supply line from the Ho Chi Minh Trail to the troops toward the coast. The sides of the mountain looked like a junkyard for choppers, as though someone with a huge broom had swept them over the edge. A rotor blade from a downed Huey had impaled itself like a huge Samurai sword into the heart of the mountainside.

Looking down on the scene, Peter suddenly felt fear well up in his stomach. He looked over at Kate, making sure she didn't notice. She leaned out the open door of the Huey busily taking pictures through a long telephoto lens, seemingly unaware of the danger that waited below.

The moment the Huey thumped down and they jumped off, two bandaged soldiers on litters were rushed toward the chopper. The pilot changed the pitch on the chopper's blades, preparing to take off before the wounded were even loaded aboard. The blades bit anxiously into the humid air and the chopper was gone in a matter of seconds.

The sound of the Huey echoed for a few seconds between the mountains. Then, when it could no longer be heard, it was replaced by the sounds of a firefight in the valley below. The steady sputtering of a deadly NVA Chicom machine gun came from a ridge directly across from where they stood, firing almost straight down toward the valley floor. Then they heard the deep beat of an American 50-caliber returning fire. Every ten seconds or so the quick cracks of M-16s and AK-47s broke the air as they spat bullets at each other. This was the firefight that had been raging for more than a month. Charlie had the Americans pinned to the floor in the narrowest section of the valley.

As they left the pad it was like they were cutting through the oppressive air of LZ Strange. Under the dark steely sky, empty ammo crates covered the scarred earth. The sandbagged bunkers around the small perimeter had been riddled with so many Vietnamese bullets that their contents had washed to the ground, mixing with the mud to form a muddy goo. The litter of war was scattered everywhere—empty C ration cans and cigarette packs and bullet-riddled jerry cans and discarded bandages. There were so many piles of empty artillery and mortar shells that it was difficult to move without tripping over them.

A soldier pointed out the way to the TOC—the Tactical Operations Center. They ducked through a small, protected opening down into a heavily fortified bunker dug deep into the reddish earth of the mountain. Inside, about ten officers and their aides were stuffed into the cramped, low-ceilinged room. The tiny crowded space, smelling of sweat and cigarette and cigar smoke, was lit only by a few naked lightbulbs pulsing from the throbs of a diesel-powered generator from dim to bright and back again. The sound of gunshots and voices under fire crackled from the bank of radios lined up on a metal field table. Then the dull thud of an exploding mortar caused the voices on the radios to stop. The voices in the room would stop along with them, waiting until someone on the radio was heard again.

Colonel Jake Broward, with an unlit cigar stuck in the corner of his mouth, stood at the table yelling into his handset, "Fuck it if Charlie is crawling right up your ass, Captain—it's time to take a shit!" He frowned when he saw Kate. Then, signing off on the radio, he addressed her. "Not language fit for a lady. But then, you're no lady, are you, honey?" He turned toward Peter and laughed, "I'll bet you know that by now, don't you, soldier?"

Kate retorted, "Speaking of gender, for such a man's man as yourself, Colonel, why is it that you find yourself in such a compromising position with the NVA?"

Broward grimaced. "We're very much in command of the situation, Miss White—I fully expect to accomplish my objective by noon tomorrow."

"You mean, by noon tomorrow, you are praying those NVA machine gunners die of heart attacks," Kate said, holding her ground.

"We're dealing with them presently, Miss White." Broward was getting mad.

"Why have you waited until now, Colonel, with so many of your troops having been virtually slaughtered?"

"We're not dealing with your candy-ass VC here." The Colonel spat out his cigar. "We've made contact with a full division of North Vietnamese regulars."

"The way it appears, Colonel—correct me if I'm wrong—is that you have lost three hundred men, dead and wounded, and six helicopters, and presently you have two companies pinned to the valley floor. Companies that I understand are decimated and cannot be rescued at the risk of losing many more men. In essence, Operation Broward County has not proved to be the easy romp on the beach you described at your briefing last week—has it, Colonel?"

Broward's huge red face, seemed to puff up even more. "Get this cunt out of my bunker before I shoot her," he screamed to his aide.

Lieutenant Zippo, ever at the ready, escorted them out through the small opening. Outside the TOC, flashing his idiotic smile, he told her,

"I think you must have understood the Colonel's message. You are not welcome here. You all have a nice day, now."

"Fuck you, Lieutenant!" Kate shot back.

Zippo's smile grew even wider, "Certainly enjoy hearing a lady's voice. Sorry to see ya go, ma'am."

Peter feared that Zippo, as crazy as he seemed, was capable of harming Kate in some way. Peter took her by the arm but she pulled away from his grip.

Glimpsing Kate's tenacity, Peter thought she might be the one to change the course of the war. He saw how her confrontation with Broward strengthened her resolve.

"Let's talk to the troops," she said, looking almost happy, as they headed back toward the chopper pad, "and get the real story."

As an army reporter, it was Peter's job to report only the "official line." He had been forced to think only in army terms. After all, he was in the army and that was his job. He'd been trained by it and brainwashed by it. He was part of it. He didn't think he could survive without it—not now, not there in the middle of Vietnam. Peter knew there was no way the army was going to allow any story to be printed that might undermine the morale of the troops. As long as he was a combat correspondent, he was expected to report battles where the only body count mentioned was Vietnamese. Reporting of friendly casualties was simply not allowed. Any story that Peter, or any of the other army correspondents, turned in made it seem that the United States was winning the war. The only publications the soldiers had access to were the ones army correspondents wrote for—Stars & Stripes, The Army Reporter, Army Digest, and the various division-and brigade-level papers—and Playboy. So the grunts in the field were made to think they were constantly kicking Charlie's ass.

As Peter walked back to the chopper pad he knew the best he could do was to help Kate get her story. Along the way they ran into a squad of grunts laying out their packs and ammo. Peter thought they wouldn't want to talk about the shit going down in the valley but he was wrong about this too. They opened up to Kate. They told her everything they knew—the truth, as they saw it.

The squad leader was a young buck sergeant who was happy to tell his story to a beautiful woman reporter. "Yes, ma'am, we have lost good men down in the valley . . . too many. Charlie is smart the way he's boxed us in, but also we're dumb for the way we got ourselves pinned down there—we walked right into his trap."

"Tell her, Sarge, about what happened." A skinny soldier looked up as he cleaned his 60-caliber with a toothbrush.

"Go on, yeah, tell 'em about that shit, Sarge," another guy chimed in. Then a third.

"We was asked to—our platoon, the Third Platoon, that is—was asked to help extract B Company. They were one of the companies that's been pinned down for a week now. They're down to nothin'."

"*Nothing* is right, man," the gunner said. "That company's down to fifteen guys. They got so many dead they can hardly move around 'em. You can see 'em all lined up on the valley floor. You can smell 'em when you get close. It makes you want to puke, man."

"They can't get to 'em because of those NVA guns," the sergeant added. "It's the truth—what Gunney's telling you. Those men of Bravo Company just walked into this trap. There's no way out for them. So far as I can see they is all going to die there unless they get a major air strike in there right away."

"It's gotta be *major*, not the usual 'tee tee' with two jets firing a couple of rockets," said the gunner. "That won't mean shit down there . . . not shit. Those guys are dug in halfway to China!"

"There's no way out at the end of the valley, Sergeant?" Kate asked him.

"No way, ma'am. Charlie's 50-cal makes it so they can't move. Charlie's got the ridge and he can see if a GI so much as scratches his ass—excuse my French. And they got mortars besides."

"Bravo was sent into deep, deep shit," another soldier added. "When we went down Charlie wouldn't let us even get close. He didn't want Bravo Company to have our help. He's starving 'em down there."

"Sure glad it ain't fuckin' *me*," said the gunner.

"Saddle up!" the sergeant called, and the men wearily stood, helping to lift their heavy gear onto each other's backs, and then they disappeared over the edge of the mountain heading off somewhere to the north— happy, Peter guessed, not to be heading directly down to the fighting.

"We've got to get down to the valley." Kate looked at him.

As they walked up to the chopper pad she said, "Broward's showing his best side now."

"I've seen it before," Peter replied.

A battle-weary old staff sergeant sat solemnly on the edge of the pad on a stack of wooden ammo crates. He looked up through his hollow eyes as they approached, and then he looked away again offering no greeting.

"Can we ride with you?" Peter asked. "We're trying to get down to the valley."

After a long pause, the sergeant replied, his eyes falling on their cameras. "Waddya want with that graveyard? All's that comes back is body bags."

"We've got orders," Peter lied.

"Lucky you. You kin ride the next bird down."

"I'll help you unload the ammo crates when we land."

"Shee-it. Ain't no way *I'm* goin' down. I ain't got no orders ta go. Have you seen the pile of helicopters lying at the bottom of this hill?" He motioned with his head toward the edge of the pad.

"We have to go," said Kate.

"She's a reporter," Peter added.

"Oh, I see." The sergeant smiled knowingly, pulling out a pack of Kools and offering them each one.

"There's some very serious shit going on down in that valley right now."

"War is a serious business, Sergeant," said Kate. "I want to find out what those men down there are killing themselves for."

"Off the record—nothing worth a shit," said the sergeant. "I can tell you that from right up here."

15

The deafening roar of a twin-rotor Chinook echoed through the fog-shrouded valley, catching the three of them by surprise as it popped up from over the other side of the LZ. It lifted up and dropped down almost on top of them—its strong prop wash nearly pushing them over the edge. The three of them had to lie flat on their stomachs behind the ammo crates while the huge ship settled down onto the pad. Two men jumped off the rear deck. With Peter and the sergeant helping, it took only a couple of minutes to load the Chinook. There was no time to second-guess whether they should go or not.

"Coming?" the crew chief asked. Once they were inside, he yelled to be heard over the engine noise, "Sit on the crates—it's the safest place."

They clambered onto the top of the pile while the crew chief joined the tail gunner on the edge of the rear door. The whine of the powerful jet engines made it impossible to talk, but it didn't seem to matter because the ride was so short. The Chinook dived down off the mountaintop heading straight for the valley floor. NVA machine guns suddenly came awake as the chopper raced down the side like a skier down a hill. From the moment they took off, the two gunners raked the ground below with bullets. From where the two correspondents sat, it was impossible to tell what was going on down on the ground. When the Chinook flared out, it hit the ground so hard Peter and Kate both thought the chopper had crashed. Even though it had been taking hits all the way down, the sturdy Chinook was not disabled. Hurriedly, they helped push the ammo crates off the back as a line of GIs eerily appeared out of the trees carrying body bags. The crew chief and the gunners pulled the bags aboard until they were lined up in neat rows like produce in a supermarket. One of the grunts delivering body bags locked eyes with Peter for an instant. The look on the guy's face spooked Peter. He appeared to be lost in space—like he had forgotten why he was there. *Lost in hell without a map,* as Marcus would say.

As soon as the deck was filled with bodies, the Chinook began a low crawl along the top of the tall grass. They felt the blast of heat from its jet engines on their faces as it tucked its nose down and roared across the valley floor, all the time taking hits from NVA guns. The men on the chopper fired back with everything they had. In the end, the chopper was one of the lucky ones that managed to escape from the valley—only because it was a Chinook and was so fast. But it seemed ironic that the NVA were trying to shoot down a chopper carrying dead bodies.

Peter pulled Kate toward the cover of the trees. He thought it strange that nobody emerged from the bush to collect the ammo. The grunts who'd delivered the bodies had disappeared. It felt like a deserted LZ.

When they reached the safety of the trees, the men were there—the faces—all lined up and freaked, with their eyes that had stared at death for too long. He started to photograph the faces he knew would burn haunting images into film. Looking through his eighty-five-millimeter telephoto, he saw their eyes up close. Eyes so powerful he had to shut his own to take the pictures. Behind them, more dead bodies in black plastic bags were lined up in neat rows waiting their turn for their one last chopper ride out.

16

Captain Hollowell, the company commander, was a tall, gaunt black man who had some odd stripes of silver running through his otherwise dark hair. His skin appeared to be hanging loosely over his big bones, like a coat too big for a hanger. His cheeks were sunken into the sides of his face. Recognizing a perfect subject when she saw one, Kate immediately stuck her Nikon uncomfortably close to him. He gazed back into her camera expressionless, through empty eyes. Peter watched her shoot a dozen shots of him and saw that his expression didn't change at all.

Kate saw the depth of his pain close up through the lens. "Will you tell us what happened?" she asked him compassionately. The captain was disarmed. She realized his need to tell his story.

"It was to be so simple . . ." He spoke slowly, tiredly. "Bravo, my company, was to sweep the valley from the east." He pointed behind them, longingly, as if he wished he could have been back up there now, in that direction, in that place, and had it to do all over again. Then his gaze fell to the ground. "We were to meet up with Alpha and Delta. They were to close in from each side. Echo was plugging the gap at the other end . . ." The captain's eyes grew more lost with each word he spoke. "The idea was so simple. We were going to push Charlie up against a wall—up against those ridges up there . . ." He looked up and across the valley like he was staring at heaven.

"What went wrong?" Kate asked.

"Oh, shit, ma'am . . . sorry for the language, I . . ." Hollowell fought back tears.

"Captain, don't worry about the language. We're in Vietnam for chrissakes." Kate smiled.

Hollowell didn't speak at first. A blank look came over his face. Very blank. Then he looked at Peter before slowly turning his head back toward Kate. It was as if he wanted to really see who it was he was talking to. "Yeah, I almost forgot where I was." It took a moment before they realized the captain was making a joke about being in Vietnam. It might have been a joke but he didn't laugh. None of them laughed.

Kate said, "Please."

Captain Hollowell's radio operator sat faithfully beside him. "Tell them, sir. The world deserves to know."

"Look, I'm going to tell you something that a captain in the army doesn't tell a civilian reporter. I'm going to tell *you* in particular because you chose to come down to this godforsaken place today. I guess you're the lucky ones.

"This is the truth of what happened. Delta Company never came down. They never swept their side of the valley . . . so that's how Charlie got his machine guns set up." He pointed to the ridge above and to the back of them. "Now, that doesn't sound like such a great big deal, right?"

Kate looked confused, "Well . . ."

"The big-deal part is they *refused* to sweep down." The captain was looking to see now if Kate understood. "But there's more than that . . . Delta Company—they radioed back that they were in position. They hadn't moved more than a few hundred meters off the LZ! They were refusing to fight, ma'am. That's the truth."

Kate looked incredulous.

"They are what got fifty of my men killed or wounded. This war stinks ma'am. And more than that, we can't win now. Truth is, Charlie's kicking our ass. And you can quote me as saying so."

"But aren't you . . . your career?"

"I *was* a career officer . . . I thought I was. Until this week. Until my men . . . this valley . . . Some things are bigger than career . . ."

His eyes trailed off into the distance. It was obvious the captain was about to lose it.

Again, Kate was comforting. "But you're a hero. You did your part . . . you did what you could."

"I was the bigger fool, ma'am."

"But . . . surely . . ."

"I got my men killed."

"They all died as heroes."

"Sir?" His radio operator interrupted. "Black Forest is calling in another air strike."

"Where?"

The RTO handed the captain a small slip of paper with the coordinates written on it.

"Shit, that's practically on top of us."

"And, sir, it's napalm."

"Well, why the hell not . . . nothing else has done the job."

"That's right, sir, let Charlie eat a hot meal."

"Tell Sergeant Good to pull the men as far back as he can. I don't want anybody getting fried."

Captain Hollowell turned back to them. "Get some good pictures," he said. "You two had better get back by the troops. You never know what to expect from Charlie when he gets napalmed. He may come running right down this mountain."

As Captain Hollowell's words trailed off into infinity, they heard the scream of the first F-4 Phantom racing down into the valley. The sound blasted into their eardrums—so loud it hurt. It was too late by the time they dove facedown onto the ground covering their ears with their hands. When the napalm exploded, the blast entered their bodies not by the ears and eyes but by shock wave first. The rockets hitting the earth shook them to the bone, rattling their brains as if they were made of glass.

The flash of pure red-yellow-orange fire was too bright to look at. It could've been called beautiful except for what it was—hot, gooey burning jelly that stuck to anything it touched. It surged ahead across the ground and through the trees, frying whatever had the bad luck to be in its way. Napalm. As quickly as the first wave of heat surrounded them, the next came. And the next. In waves, one within the other, like waves on the ocean—only with the energy of heat.

After the second plane made its pass, Charlie popped up from his spider hole again blasting the trees all around the Americans. His bullets whistled just inches over their heads. Peter was sure he could hear him laughing.

Kate and Peter's eyes met. "I'd like to get inside his head for a little while," she said, referring to the NVA. "He knows how not to give up. He knows how to survive."

"Do you think he'll win the war?" Peter asked her. It seemed at first, like a strange place to ask such a question, and then on second thought, he realized it was the perfect place.

"I think he will," she answered. "I think he already has."

Kate held out her hand to the captain, who smothered it between his huge palms. "What happened to Delta Company? Where are they now?" she asked him.

"Don't know. Don't matter now . . ."

The radio squawked to life. Colonel Broward's voice could be heard over the static.

"Ask him," said Hollowell.

From the small radio speaker, Broward shouted a stream of barely intelligible profanities. Hollowell's eyes suddenly came to life as he reached for the radio, angrily changing the frequency dial.

"Don't need any more dead or wounded." Hollowell spoke softly, cutting off Broward's transmission.

They were all in awe of Hollowell's bravery. They knew the captain's simple action to be the ultimate protest in war. It was mutiny.

The captain, his radio operator, and the two reporters sat silently in their small unprotected place on the floor of the A Shau Valley with the biggest question anyone could ask about the war in Vietnam rattling around in their heads—"Do we keep on fighting?" All four of them knew the consequences of Hollowell's action. Three of the four felt undeniably proud of the company commander. Hollowell, himself, was somewhere far beyond pride.

They all heard the sound of a chopper in the distance. First they heard it land on LZ Strange far above them. Then take off again. For a few seconds there was quiet, then the chopper roared down the side of the valley wall. Finally they heard it land close by where they sat on the valley floor. They remained silent, waiting, all the time knowing who it was.

Colonel Broward, red-faced and angry, burst through the leaves like King Kong dressed in fatigues. "What the fuck is going on here, Captain?"

Hollowell stood up, in his own time. "Yes, sir?"

"Your radio's out?"

"Why . . . no, sir. She's working just fine."

"What!" Broward screamed.

Hollowell spoke softly, "I said, she's working just fine, sir."

"Check the frequency, Lieutenant," Broward ordered Zippo.

Zippo bent down beside the radio, "It's set to the wrong frequency, sir."

"You fuck!" Broward glared at Hollowell. "You skinny nigger fuck. You're relieved of your command, Captain. As of this moment."

Captain Hollowell remained in place, impassively.

Broward turned toward Kate who stood beside Hollowell. The colonel, unable to control his anger toward her, planted both hands around her neck. "You cunt! You rotten fucking cunt!" He threw her down.

Peter, almost couldn't believe what he was seeing. But he reacted and lunged at Broward, grabbing his neck in a stranglehold, wrestling him to the ground.

"No, Peter! Don't!" Kate yelled.

Peter stopped to look up at her, incredulous. Zippo helped the colonel up. Broward screamed into Kate's face. "You dumb fuck! You know you're trying to get yourself killed! But don't do it in my fucking valley! *I'll* kill you first!"

While Broward was screaming, Peter began to understand. He looked Kate in the eye. But Broward turned to him. "Sergeant Hill, I'm going to see that you're fucked, royally, for bringing her out here. I can promise you, it won't be a simple court-martial either." Peter got a close-up view into Broward's eyes and what Peter saw was frightening. He thought that if the eyes are the windows to the soul he was looking at a man with no soul. Broward's being was consumed with hate. Hate and anger. "I'm gonna send you someplace where you can't come back!"

Then he turned to Hollowell. "I'm taking command of your company, Captain," Broward said. "I'm going to end this fucking debacle, now. I'm gonna show you assholes how it's done." As he spoke, the high-pitched roar of two F-4 Phantom jets echoed through the valley. Broward's face quickly lit up in ecstasy. "Sit back and watch the show . . ."

Within seconds, the first jet swept down the valley no more than thirty meters from the ground—much lower than the air strike they'd just witnessed. As the plane passed in front of them, it dropped its full pay-load of napalm. Two rockets detached from under the plane's wing, shooting like javelins through the thick jungle on the opposite side of the valley. This time, they saw the bombs roll. What was left of the vegetation on the ground lit up. Again, the heat was searing. As fast as the jet came it was gone, disappearing up into the cloud cover. A second jet followed the path of the first and again the hillside burst into bright red-orange flames. Broward shouted with glee like a little boy who'd just opened his first Christmas present.

A North Vietnamese soldier popped up from just behind a ridge only about twenty-five meters in front of the Americans and came running across the valley floor. He stunned everyone. For one thing, he was so close. Nobody fired at him at first. He was in flames, his clothes, his hair, his flesh. He had no weapon in his hands. Instead, he was a human torch, running like some crazed kamikaze pilot, directly at them. A soldier beside Peter fired straight at the man's chest. Though the man was riddled with bullets, somehow he kept running. Peter held up his M-16, aimed directly at the man, and fired a single shot at his face. The bullet violently snapped his head back. He fell backward in a burst of flames on the grass about ten meters in front of them. As he writhed agonizingly in the grass, they watched him turn into char. Peter and the other soldier fired the remainder of their bullets at the man again—to put him out of his agony.

Kate grabbed Peter's arm. She knew what he had done. She knew that even when he had fired the first time, he was not killing a Vietnamese, he was shooting because he felt sorry for the man. Something Peter had learned about himself—each time he had shot at a Vietnamese, it felt different. Usually it was out of fear, but this time it had been different again.

Peter was overwhelmed by what had happened. He wanted to leave. Kate was confused. She realized that she might be falling in love with a nineteen-year-old soldier—a soldier still very young for nineteen. She didn't want it to happen. She determined not to let it. She pushed the thought out of her mind thinking only about furthering the story she had come for, the one that could make her career.

17

They hitched a ride out on a dust-off chopper that came in to extract a badly wounded soldier from Hollowell's company. The young soldier lay stretched out on the floor at their feet. A medic held a blood-soaked bandage against the soldier's head while the chopper raced above the treetops on the way to the Ninety-third Medevac Hospital in Chu Lai. The bandage was made of a few strips of fatigue cloth cut from his shirt. Even with the medic pressing it, the blood leaked out from underneath, running in rivers down his neck and shoulders and across his chest. For some reason Peter couldn't keep his eyes off him, watching the dark rivers of blood feeding into the pools on the floor. The pools were becoming ponds, their surfaces vibrating from the motion of the Huey's blades chopping against the air. The scene became a vision to Peter and the vision became unreal. Peter wanted to lean forward in his seat to press the soldier's head between his hands, to stop the bleeding. But the rivers ran much too fast. How much blood did a man contain? he wondered. Was it quarts or only pints? When was he going to run out?

As if he was writing the story the way he wanted to, Peter searched for the right words. Listening to the small voice inside his head he knew that *man* was not the correct word at all. The soldier was a boy—

a boy just like *he* was. He knew this was why the scene was so horrible to him.

Why didn't the medic do more to help the boy? The medic just stared out the open door seeming not to care.

Peter felt hopeless.

The jungle ended abruptly. Suddenly they were flying in cooler air across a transparent green sea. Peter looked away from the soldier and down at the wave that followed them just a few meters below the chopper. The wave was continuous. It rolled forward at the same speed as the chopper—which seemed to be some sort of odd coincidence of nature. How could this be, that a wave could flow more than a hundred miles an hour? Peter thought he might be losing his mind. The soldier bled, the wave flowed. There was just too much going on that he couldn't explain. There was never enough time to ask the questions that could provide the answers. He had no choice but to let go.

Perhaps his thought had been wrong. Perhaps he was no longer a boy.

It was as if he had bought tickets to a movie he could not leave, no matter how horrible the show.

As the chopper approached Chu Lai, Kate, who had been silent during the entire flight, decided to speak. She leaned close to Peter's ear. Stuck in thoughts that ran deep, at first he only half heard her. "Peter, Jake and I had an affair, four years ago, when I first came in-country. Jake helped me find my way. You could say I used him, I suppose. Later I found out how horrible he was. He's a beast."

Peter realized it was Broward she was talking about, but it seemed so unimportant now. He continued to look down at the water. Kate wasn't telling him anything he didn't already know. He turned to look at her but no words came. He wasn't angry, he wasn't *not* angry. He felt, in a funny way, that he'd lost his mind somewhere in the past few hours. Where he'd lost it, he wasn't sure. If he had known, he'd be able to retrieve it again. All he knew for sure was that the world was spinning, faster and faster. He wasn't sure he could keep up anymore. He wasn't sure he wanted to.

As Kate continued to try to make him understand, it was like he was outside himself listening to her words. "I told you . . . he helped me," her voice spoke but her words meant nothing to him.

Peter turned his head to look outside the chopper again, trying to focus on the turquoise sea. But he felt like he wasn't really looking out at all. He was looking at a world contained inside himself. He pictured himself flying right off the surface of the earth as it spun—being catapulted out into deep space. After all, they'd heard, only the day before, that a man had walked on the moon . . .

Peter thought about that to keep his mind off the soldier. The headline on the *Stars & Stripes* was MAN WALKS ON MOON. Peter read the story sitting in a lawn chair outside the photo lab. It was night and he followed the words with a flashlight. The moon, like it was posing for him, hung in the sky like someone had hung it up there. Peter didn't believe the story. He treated it as though it was an article in a tabloid. From where he sat in that strange corner of the world, it seemed totally impossible. All he knew was, that he was thankful for the moon when it was full. Like the saying went: *Full moon tonight—Charlie won't fight!* But a man walking up there . . . no way in hell. Even the pictures in the paper looked fake.

The Huey tilted toward the beach and for a few seconds Peter was facing straight down. Kate grabbed his arm as if to keep him from falling out. Peter knew he wouldn't fall. He thought of his first chopper ride in training back at Fort Jackson where the instructor demonstrated by placing a glass of water beside the door. No matter how hard the pilot tried, he couldn't spill the water out of the glass, let alone make the glass fall from the chopper.

The Huey slid upward a few hundred feet up into the sky, before it settled down quickly onto the big red cross in the center of the Ninety-third Evac Hospital pad. Two surgeons rushed out for the wounded soldier. Peter and Kate remained frozen in their seats while the surgeons took the soldier's vital signs right inside the chopper. Peter wondered why they didn't know, as he did, just by looking at the boy. After they had lifted the body up, it seemed like the boy had left all his blood on the chopper floor. The pool of red shone in the sun like the surface of a freshly waxed car. The doctors put the dead soldier on a litter and walked toward the hospital door. The pilot shut down the engine and the crew chief walked to the edge of the pad, turning on a hose.

For some reason Peter reached for his wallet to make sure he still had the picture—the one he always carried, where he stood leaning on the side of his Ford station wagon. He remembered that he'd waxed it four times before his sister had taken the picture. Four coats of wax.

18

Kate leaned back—exhausted, disheveled—against the plywood wall at the correspondents' phone in the division PIO. She was talking to Randy in Saigon. "Read that back to me—would you? No, no, we can't say that. Not yet. We don't know where Delta Company was, or is, even now. We have to find them."

Kate believed it was the beginning of the end. The war couldn't continue if soldiers refused to fight. But that had to be proven. And she had to show that it was not only an isolated case. She knew how good the army was at covering things up. She needed to dig in more places.

As Kate spoke into the phone, Peter began to caress her neck. He wanted nothing more than to be lost inside her. At that moment he didn't care who she was. She was a body, which was enough. Kate felt exactly the same. He unbuttoned her shirt and bent down to kiss her breasts. It didn't seem to occur to either of them that they were in a public place. They were oblivious to the existence of a world beyond them. Their brains had been filled to overflowing with images that flashed crazily, in no particular order. Hollowell, the dead soldier in the dust-off chopper, treetops, the turquoise sea. Neither of them wanted to replay the movie anymore.

Kate still had to finish calling the story in. "Perhaps you can find out

something in Saigon at the press briefing tomorrow morning." She kissed
the top of Peter's head. "I'll be in Saigon tomorrow."

Peter quickly undid the buttons on Kate's fatigue pants. He kneeled
down to kiss her stomach.

Kate continued to talk on the phone. "I'm just happy to be out of the
line of fire. I'm . . ." He stood up, unbuttoned his fly and entered her,
pressing her up against the plywood wall. Kate went on, ". . . tomorrow,
yes, oh yes . . . I will . . ." Finally, she hung up the phone. Peter rammed
himself against her—using the bone in his groin as a sort of weapon. Kate
pulled him against her, coaxing him to move faster and push deeper into
her. She reached her hand down to her clitoris, rubbing her middle finger madly across it, pressing harder than she ever had until she reached
an orgasm that made her scream. Peter bit into her ear when he came.
He tasted her blood. They fell back against the plywood wall and slid,
exhausted, to the floor. They sat side by side, not even bothering to pull
their clothes back on.

They looked into each other's eyes, not at all surprised at the heat of
their passion.

Only when they heard footsteps coming down the hall did they pull
up their pants. Kate had just finished buttoning up her shirt when a PIO
sergeant walked into the room. "Am I disturbing you?"

"No, not at all, Sergeant." Kate smiled. "We're finished here."

19

Maybe it was the beautiful turquoise color they'd seen from the helicopter. Maybe it was the clarity of it—the transparency—that drew them toward it. Perhaps they felt it would purify them or wash away their sins. Maybe they thought if they just gave in to it, submerging their bodies completely within its cool molecules they'd be rejuvenated or even reborn. Suddenly the sea became the glorious South China Sea. It had never been *glorious* before.

They walked down to the beach where the stand downs were held—where, even in Vietnam, it was possible to go body surfing or snorkeling or even waterskiing. There was a small grass-roofed hut where they signed out snorkeling equipment—masks and snorkels and swim fins.

They sat on the edge of the foam where the powdery white sand slid down into the waves. They had carried a bottle of tequila with them. They took turns drinking from the bottle, which had started to work its magic under the bright sun. They sat down on the burning hot sand. It felt good when the next wave pushed some cool water up under them. They fit their feet into blue swim fins. Kate tightened the straps around the heels and Peter stole a look between her legs. Kate wore Peter's T-shirt instead of a bathing suit. He looked at the place where the inside of her thighs seemed to disappear—where they slipped into the hidden world in the shadow beneath the edge of the olive drab shirt. A few hairs from between her legs were just barely visible. A wave broke on the sand pushing some sea foam up under her shirt. He wondered if the water felt good to her.

"Ohhh." She turned her head and gave him a wet tequila kiss. "Did *that* feel good!"

They adjusted the straps on their masks, spitting on the inside of the glass just the way Peter had seen Jacques Cousteau do it on television. They didn't talk much. There was nothing left to say. They only wanted the simple experience of floating in the cleansing temple of the sea.

To the far left, where the beach looked like a ship heading out to sea, the palm trees grew so close to the water that the waves washed right up into their roots. Beneath the trees a wall of coral formed the peninsula, creating one of the points of a nearly perfect crescent. At the top of the coral hill the Officers' Club dangled precariously.

With their flippers on, the two of them waddled like ducks backward into the water, pointing their butts into the waves. They each took a last gulp of tequila before Peter was ready to let go of the bottle. He chucked it up onto the beach. Kate pulled off the T-shirt Peter had given her, made it into a wet ball, and threw it up on the sand. Peter decided to take off his suit, which got snagged when he tried to pull it over his flippers. The cool water felt good against his skin. They swam out together along the edge of the coral reef, keeping a safe distance from where the waves were smashing against the rock. The view underwater through the swim masks was overwhelming. As they dove down, schools of thousands of tiny fish surrounded them, making tunnels that Kate and Peter swam through. Each school was different—some were of bright colors, reds and greens and bright yellow. In one school the fish were transparent. There were plants that grew from holes in the coral—bright green flowerlike vegetation with tendrils that danced with the movement of the invisible waves beneath the surface. They felt they were visiting a world that belonged to other creatures, not to them.

This was the happiest moment Peter could remember since he'd arrived in-country. Heading out into deeper water, it was as if they had crossed an imaginary line where they became part of the *rest* of the world—the world that was *not Vietnam*. Peter had to remind himself that the rest of the world was at peace. It seemed it was where the waves broke against the sharp and dangerous coral that Vietnam—and its civil war—began. Peter made a mental note, which he tucked away somewhere safe, that if he ever decided to make an escape, he would do it by sea. After all, he had just realized, it took only a single dive to be out of the evil country into neutral territory. Who knows, maybe he'd build a sailboat someday and sail away . . .

It was at that moment of blissfulness that the shark appeared. It happened when he and Kate had just passed a huge outcropping of coral. They had just swum around a corner of the reef headed into a deep blue bowl where the bottom suddenly dropped off and the sea turned far deeper—and colder. He was huge and evil looking. He moved with harsh, quick, predetermined jolts that put him in command of the place. Without warning he darted quickly at Kate, who swam in front of Peter. At the last second he veered off. Kate stopped. Treading water with her swim fins kept her standing upright in the water. She went up for a breath of air, the top of her head breaking the surface, but she never took her eyes off the shark. As she breathed through the snorkel, she kept her movements fluid, as nearly motionless as she could. Peter was about ten meters behind her watching helplessly as the shark circled all the way around her. He swam between them, coming within only a few meters or so of her back.

Peter's thoughts froze in his brain. *What if he . . . what if she . . .*

Then the shark turned and, with a flash of his tail, swam away.

They watched as he became small and harmless, finally disappearing into the deep blue beneath them.

20

They rode together in the battered old PIO jeep, headed north along the dirt highway between Chu Lai and Tam Ky. The monsoon rains had let up and the sun was bright and hot. Kate tied a black silk bandanna around her forehead to keep the sweat from her eyes. Peter carved his way around the puddles in the road and the swarms of Vietnamese, like bees brought out by the sun, hawking their wares along the roadside. Reaching the village of Tam Ky, they ran into a long convoy of ARVN trucks blocking the road. They were told the first truck had struck and killed an old woman carrying firewood. Her wood had been scattered across the road and children were making off with the sticks while the pompous ARVN soldiers in their well-starched uniforms stood beside their trucks smoking American cigarettes posing for invisible cameras. As Peter maneuvered the jeep around the dead woman, he said to Kate, "Forgotten casualty."

"I'm sure she's got a story," she replied.

"But can you write them all?" he asked.

The question stopped Kate in her tracks. She thought for a minute before she spoke. "If you write one story, that's enough. It includes her—includes a lot of others like her," she said finally.

A South Vietnamese policeman, trying to sort things out, flagged their jeep past the convoy. There were about fifty brand-new two-and-a-half-ton trucks, all empty, stopped in the road.

"Wonder what the ARVNs are up to?" Kate asked herself out loud.

"No fucking good." Peter answered her question for her.

About two kilometers past the accident, Peter turned off the highway onto a small dirt road and headed west toward the highlands. It was a narrow path of a road, verdant and beautiful, kept cool by the overhanging trees. Beyond the narrow line of trees on both sides of the road, the rice paddies had turned a piercing bright green from the monsoon rains. This was the color of Vietnam Peter loved. The green in Vietnam was brighter than any green he'd ever seen.

"It's so beautiful here," Kate said. "Thank you, Peter."

"For what?"

"For bringing me here."

After rounding a long curve, a solitary white stucco building with an orange tiled roof was visible a few hundred meters away at the end of the road. The modest structure sat in the shade of a grove of tall palms arching over its roof as if they were protecting it from something—from the war.

Kate touched Peter's shoulder. "Let's stop here and walk the rest of the way. It's so quiet. Let's not spoil it."

Peter pulled off the road beneath one of the palm trees. He locked the steering wheel with a chain and padlock while Kate stood beside the jeep taking a picture of the temple with a telephoto lens. Then they walked to the building beside one another, silent, not holding hands. As they approached, Peter pointed to the ideograms painted above the door. Kate took a picture then tucked her camera into her canvas shoulder bag. Peter pushed open the heavy wooden door.

Inside, the temple was empty. It was silent and the air was still. There were no seats, only a clean white marble floor contained within its cool whitewashed stucco walls. A small ceramic statue of Buddha looked down on the room from an altar at the far end. Beneath the statue, small pots in a line were filled with sand in which sticks of incense had been burned. The few sticks that were still smoking filled the room with the sweet fragrance of sandalwood. The room seemed to be a container filled with silence.

Kate took his Peter's hand and led him up to the altar. "I want to make an offering," she said.

They sat cross-legged on the cool floor, where Kate picked up a stick of incense from a basket beneath the altar, lit it with matches left on the altar, and stuck it in a pot at Buddha's feet. Tears ran down her cheeks.

"Something strange happens to me in places like this—I start to come apart. If I had the time, I'd try to get myself together."

"You seem to me to be quite together."

"If you only knew!" She took a deep breath and wiped away her tears. "For me, being in Vietnam is a fucked-up sort of fantasy."

"Fantasy!" he exclaimed. "How can you say that? It's so real. So fucking real! Real ground, real grass, real wet rain, real fucking heat! How fucking real can you get? If I knew how real this place was, I wouldn't have come . . . If only I had known what Vietnam was like . . ." He paused to think, then said, "But I met you."

"But you don't know me, Peter. You really don't know who I am. I'm so fucked up. I'm afraid if you really knew me . . ."

Peter placed his palm gently over her mouth.

Kate pulled his hand away. "Do you want to know what Buddha said?" she asked. "All sorrows, which appear . . . in great variety here, all originate from what is dear. And if there's nothing dear, do not arise . . ."

Peter listened intently, impressed at Kate's knowledge. She continued. "If you aspire to be sorrowless, do not hold anything dear in this world . . ."

"You will never fall in love?" he asked her, thinking as soon as he'd said the words, they sounded so dumb.

"I want to tell you a secret, " she said softly. "Something I've never told anyone."

He watched her eyes grow even larger. He felt as he looked into them, that he could get lost inside her—as if there was a deep, dark jungle to explore or maybe a series of hidden tunnels. Not wanting to go there, he switched his focus to her skin instead—to the tiny lines in the corners of her eyes. The lines, he decided, that were the worldly evidence of the depth of suffering that remained hidden within Kate. He felt his heart start to pound, afraid of what Kate was about to say. But he knew that if he was going to let himself feel for Kate he would have to let himself listen. It seemed that Kate's secret was something she desperately needed to drag out of the darkness.

She gripped his hand tightly as if she was hanging on to something of this world while she looked back into the frightening world of her past.

"You have to promise," she began, "you can never . . . oh, that sounds so stupid. It's just that I have always wanted to tell someone and never trusted anyone enough to know . . . oh God, I don't know if I can say it . . . maybe there's no need . . . maybe I'll just have to die with it . . ."

Kate stopped. Peter saw the muscles in her jaw tense up beneath her tanned skin.

He kissed her on the forehead. "It's up to you. Do whenever you want. I can't tell you what to do."

She cut him off. "You don't know how bad it is."

"You're right—I don't."

"I want this to be something that will stay in this temple forever." She looked deep into his eyes. "It feels like I've had to come here—to Vietnam, to this temple, to meet you . . . all these things had to happen first, for me to be able to even think of telling someone—to be able to tell you."

Kate leaned toward Peter and whispered softly in his ear. As he listened, he closed his eyes so he could imagine himself totally within her world.

After she had told him, he pressed his lips against her hair, feeling again as if he wanted to crawl inside her with his M-16 to kill her pain. But he knew there was nothing he could do for her but listen.

"Let's say a prayer," he said.

"To Buddha," she added.

They leaned forward on their knees touching their foreheads to the floor. The temple was silent except for the moments when Kate's loud sobs burst into the cool air like explosions. Finally she bolted upright. "I feel so ashamed . . . so utterly filled with shame . . . having told you."

He looked at her not knowing what to say, but he heard himself speak. "It's horrible what happened, Kate. I know that. But it happened a long time ago. It's over."

She jumped up to her feet and burst out angrily, "That's just it, Peter, it isn't over! It's never fucking over! I can't forget. I can't ever forget— not for one minute of one fucking day!" She stopped. Her voice grew softer when she said, "I think it's what brought me to fucking Vietnam in the first place. Don't you think that could be it?"

He stood up beside her knowing there was nothing he could say. Because the truth was that he didn't know have any answer. He didn't want to say the wrong thing. It was at that moment that he realized how much he loved her.

He reached out to hold her, but she backed away. He remained looking at her, as she once again sank inside herself, her eyes staring down at the white marble floor. He realized something else at that moment—that it was impossible for one human to feel another's pain.

He wasn't exactly sure why he did but he took Kate's hand and placed a tarnished old Vietnamese coin in her palm—a piaster he'd been carrying in his pocket for good luck. He folded her fingers over the coin to make sure it didn't drop.

"What's this for?" she asked.

"You gave me something to keep—this is yours to keep." It sounded so sappy, he thought. He couldn't believe what was happening to him— he was turning soft.

"Peter, I'll save it—for always." As she spoke the word *always* she frowned. It sounded long ago and far away. He put his hands on her shoulders holding her at arm's length—taking a long look at the re-markable woman he was with. He moved his thumb across her fore-head wiping away her frown. Then he pulled her close to him. Closing his eyes, he held her in his arms—feeling for the first time how frail she really was.

He could feel Kate's struggle with herself—the way she would let go and then pull back. The way she would open for a second then close—almost like breathing. He was content to hold her close to him, his head tucked in against her neck. He breathed her in, inhaling the moist fragrance of her skin. When he opened his eyes and her ear was an inch away, he saw something so fragile about it, this listening de-vice that had heard so much cruelty. For some reason, he wasn't sure why, he grabbed a handful of Kate's thick hair, clenching it as if to tell her he was holding on—he wasn't going to let her go, not to a place where she might fade into some lost memory.

He knew, when Kate let him pull her hair without complaint, that it made her feel good. Grabbing a handful in his fist, he pulled it until he knew it hurt. He knew she loved the pain. She looked directly into his eyes and smiled, to tell him it was okay. The pain was something that made the moment tangible, physical, for her. It brought her out of herself. Otherwise she would be forced to remain lost in the world inside her head. What Kate secretly wished was for Peter to pull her hair even harder. She wished he would drag her around the temple on the floor. She wished . . .

Kate's frailty was strange to Peter, but he was getting used to strange. Oddly, her weakness made him feel stronger, like it made him more of a man. He tightened his fist, gripping Kate's hair even tighter, and gave it one last strong tug, nearly to the point where it could've pulled out at the roots. He did it knowing that he had granted Kate's wish.

21

The sun shown brightly through the window in Gisella's office. Even across the room, where Peter leaned back into the soft center of the couch, he felt the sun's heat on his chest.

"So, after she told you, you shared her secret with her," Gisella spoke seriously. "That's a big thing—knowing something so important about someone."

Peter was angry that Gisella was trying to get him to tell Kate's secret—to say it out loud—which he never would. It made him uncomfortable to think of Gisella analyzing Kate. He turned the direction of the conversation back to him. "Being with Kate made me feel strong," he told her, "I felt like I was growing more powerful."

"Maybe at that moment in the temple you changed—could that be?" Peter watched Gisella smile. It was a friendlier and less businesslike smile than he'd seen before. It was as if she was truly happy for him. "There are moments in life when we do change, when we go through transformations."

He felt happy. Thinking back to that moment with Kate, it did seem to be one of those rare times during the war when he had reached a kind of plateau. "Are you saying I had a breakthrough? In the temple? In fucking Vietnam?"

Gisella smiled a satisfied smile.

"Maybe you're right, Gisella, maybe I did actually learn a fucking thing or two in Nam. But if you want to know the truth, I think that it's *now* that I'm learning. Not when I was there. It was like I was unconscious or some fucking thing—the entire fucking time I was in Vietnam."

"I think perhaps you just don't remember. Isn't it possible, when you were there, you were conscious, and then afterward, over the years, you have forgotten?"

"Maybe."

Gisella smiled.

"You know, when I first came to you and you asked me about Vietnam, I couldn't remember anything. Okay—maybe three things. Remember? I couldn't even remember Kate."

"Yes."

"Yes? That's all you have to say?" Peter felt his anger getting the better of him. It brought him back to the reason he'd come to Gisella in the first place—his anger. Even before the drinking came the anger. Whenever the anger surfaced she had taught him to try to think of what it was masking. What was it he was afraid of?

Peter leaned forward with his elbows on his knees propping his chin in his hands. "What's amazing is that I even forgot the beautiful things— the good things. I can understand blotting out the bad shit, but why the good things? There were some great moments."

"Exactly, " she smiled.

Peter stared out the window for a moment. "Why does it happen?" he said softly.

"What? "

"Why did I forget?" He turned toward Gisella.

She was about to answer when he answered the question for himself. "If you can't remember something it's like it never happened."

22

The light outside the temple was so bright it hurt their eyes. Kate
pulled a pair of gold-rimmed military sunglasses from her camera
bag. An old mama san squatted in the shade beside the temple wall
with a basket of fruits—mangos, coconuts, and small bananas.

"My stomach's talking," said Kate.

"What's it saying?"

"Bananas."

Peter paid the mama san five piasters for a dozen of the tiny bananas,
far more than the going rate. Kate quickly peeled one. "Mmmh, sweet!"
She smiled.

"Like you."

"Like me? I'm a lot of things, Peter, but sweet is not one of them."

"I disagree—you're very sweet. I've tasted you, remember?"

"Sweet of you to say so."

He smiled at her, his face stuffed with banana. "Very sweet."

After leaving the temple, the two of them talked of bananas and
their favorite fruits and not much else as they walked back to the jeep.
Peter undid the chain and lock on the steering wheel and they headed
back toward Tam Ky. Once they were driving, neither of them had a
desire to talk. Both of them, it seemed, were content just to take in the
beauty of the countryside. The bright sun filtered through the tall

palm trees that hung over the road like giant umbrellas, the shadows from their branches laying cool gray patterns on top of the warm gold of the sandy road. To Kate it seemed as if they were riding a chariot along a path of gold. The overload of emotion seemed to have been re-placed, for both of them, with a crystal-clear vision. It was like being on drugs, thought Peter.

23

Peter's wife Nina followed him up a leaf-covered trail, part of the nature preserve, three hundred acres of land East Millbank set aside for hikes. They had been married for sixteen years, having met in California in 1970 the year after Peter returned from Vietnam. They were both hippies at the time. The army had released Peter early—for medical reasons, they said—immediately after his arrival in Ft. Lewis, Washington. A PIO sergeant from Americal Headquarters had tracked him down, after he'd been missing for more than a month, hiding out at the Buddhist temple where he'd sought *spiritual asylum*. The sergeant, a tall, thin black man named Oscar, had driven out along the Tam Ky Road, stopping to ask the villagers along the way if they'd seen a lone American soldier in a jeep. Some young boys had seen his jeep parked behind the small temple at the end of the road—the white temple that the VC never bothered.

Peter and Nina had met on a commune in Creswell, Oregon, about twenty miles south of the college town of Eugene. Nina had been living on a farm—a picturesque place called "Coyote Creek"—with her two horses and about ten artists and craftspeople whose main occupations served to bring them just enough wherewithal to keep them stoned on organic hallucinogens—peyote and mescaline, pot and hash. Nina had stopped in her Volkswagen bus, her boyfriend David stoned and asleep in the back, to give Peter a ride. He couldn't hide his military haircut at the time although his beard had begun to grow out. According to Nina, she *knew* the moment she saw him. She had told Peter years later that her first impression of him was of a man who was capable of action. Both of them, for some odd reason, distinctly remember the sound of the tires crunching on the gravel as she pulled onto the shoulder of the highway. Peter also remembers that it took her about a hundred yards to stop the van. He always wondered if it was her metabolism slowed by the use of drugs or just poor brakes. Nina had felt an odd feeling in her stomach as Peter swung onto the bench seat beside her. From the start, they couldn't take their eyes off each other. Nina, contrary to the other women on the farm who didn't seem to bathe, kept herself clean and well groomed. Her long blond tresses were neatly braided—the way she had worn her hair since she had been given her first pony on her fifth birthday. She was a strong and able woman who had been used to being the decision maker in her two-year relationship with David, whom she'd met at the University of Oregon in Eugene. David, who stayed stoned virtually all his waking hours, bought his dope with the money he made from making candles. By the time Peter came into her life, Nina was doing drugs less and less often. She was also tiring of communal life that had started out with such great promise but had, over the space of a few months, disintegrated into endless bickering over simple issues—things like who was going to empty the garbage and clean the toilets. Then she met this capable man, just returned from Vietnam, who quickly proved strong and reliable in all the ways that David wasn't. Peter intrigued Nina enough to inspire her to move David out of her bed and let him in. And probably because of the free-love culture they were living in at the time, it happened all in the space of two days. In another time and place it would've been a much slower process or it might never have happened at all.

In the crowded farmhouse, Peter was invited to sleep on the floor of their bedroom, and after David had nodded off for the evening, she had crawled naked out of her bed and onto the floor, where she seduced him. When David awakened in the morning, he found Nina curled up

in a sleeping bag with Peter on the floor. The two of them left the commune together the next day—she having sold both her horses for four
hundred dollars, enough money for gas and food to bring them back
east to Connecticut. There, they were going to get jobs "without selling out in any way at all."

They settled in East Millbank because Peter had grown up there
and knew people who might give them work. At first Peter worked as a
carpenter for a contractor friend of his father. He was making enough
money to buy all the liquor he wanted. He was drinking a case of beer
a day, smoking pot at lunchtime, and always staying stoned on week-
ends. He was going on benders of drugs and alcohol that left him in various places—asleep at the wheel of his pickup truck in the middle of a
field, in a fight at the Hideaway Inn, or even, a few times, in jail. In the
1970s, being a Vietnam veteran worked against him. Even in the small
town of East Millbank, there was little sympathy for the young boys
who'd gone off to fight in that screwed-up war. Especially for a preppy
like Peter who'd blown his chances for a degree from Yale, as his de-
tractors liked to say.

Eventually, when his drinking began to affect his work and he was
fired, he landed a job at the *East Millbank Crier* selling advertising space.
Then, when the sports reporter retired, he took over his job. Eventually,
because of the quality of his writing and because there was no one else
who was better, he was named managing editor. Peter's drinking didn't
interfere much with his work at the paper. He was able to keep it hidden
for the most part. Anyway, drinking was a badge of pride among the people at the *Crier* as it is among newspaper people everywhere. By the time
he was promoted to the top job, Peter was drinking mostly vodka. His
drinking had progressed to the point where he began the day with a drink
and then was forced to maintain this routine throughout the day. He kept
a bottle in his bottom desk drawer, which everyone knew about and nobody thought unusual. He kept a backup hidden behind his gray filing
cabinet and another stashed behind the seat of his Ford pickup. A lot of
people at the paper drank—especially the guys on the late-night shift in

the production and composing rooms. Whenever there was a late-breaking story, one that would take a full night's worth of work, Peter stayed the night more for the opportunity to drink than to work. The night a wealthy heiress was found dead in her burning Mercedes behind the supermarket Peter drank with the boys in production until early the next morning when the paper went to press. For Peter, nights like that brought back some of the excitement of Vietnam—an experience he didn't have much chance of reliving in the Connecticut countryside.

He didn't talk about Vietnam. Only rarely did he acknowledge he was a Vietnam veteran. It was not a subject he felt comfortable with. He heard later that a few times when he'd had way too much to drink, he had told some bizarre stories—one about a tribe of Aborigines he'd found living in the fuselage of an old airplane. But having been in a blackout of some sort he didn't remember telling the story. Most people didn't have a clue that he'd been to Vietnam. When people found out they usually thought he appeared much too young to have been there. It was only at home, where he felt safe enough, that his experiences would sometimes bubble up to the surface.

Nina worked as a riding instructor for a small stable where the children of wealthy insurance executives from Hartford boarded their horses. She, too, was promoted to manager and then she was asked to buy into the business and so she became half owner.

When they were first living together, they agreed that they weren't ready for marriage or children and this attitude held both things off for years. What kept them close during those early years was probably the fact that they both had lived through major traumas. For Nina, it had been the breakup of her family and death of her father of a heart attack at an early age. For Peter it was Vietnam.

Now, so many years later, when Nina and Peter walked, there was no desire for either of them to communicate. They were content to exist within their own private worlds. They had learned to live together, but separately. They occupied the same house but were consumed, most of the time, by different agendas—Peter with his writing and editing, Nina with the children and her job managing the stables. Each of them was careful not to intrude on the other's personal space because, when that happened, it would cause a fight and it was always the same fight replayed with the same result.

But as they walked, they knew how to share certain thoughts. Having been together for so long, they no longer needed to say things out loud. Most of the communication that passed between them was silently understood. They had become trusted companions, aware of each other's needs. Although much of their early passion had subsided, it would be wrong not to call what ran between them love. They had been protective and faithful allies to each other throughout their marriage.

After a few years, Peter's memory of Kate faded. He hardly had thought of her at all after his return to the States and then any memory of her disappeared altogether.

24

"I want you to see something," Peter said to Kate, turning the jeep off the shady road onto another that headed north. They passed a woman with her children gathering firewood along the roadside. After a few minutes' drive, now in the hot sun, they arrived at the bank of the Song Tra Bong River. Peter stopped the jeep and led Kate down to the edge of the water. The river was shallow and just beginning to widen into the delta. From where they stood it looked about half a kilometer across. The sun sparkling on the tiny wind ripples on the water's surface created a dazzling effect. A few hundred meters downriver lay what was left of a railroad bridge that had once spanned the river in five separate sections. What remained was nothing but an abstract sculpture, a hulk of twisted iron, four of the five sections having settled into the water. The black metal was bent as if it were made of dough, not iron. Its huge beams turned into arcs that curved in and out of the river. Sitting along the single section still in place was a row of children holding bamboo poles, their long lines dangling into the shallow water. The scene put Peter in awe of the immense power of the war's destruction. The first time he'd seen it, he'd been so moved by the power of the place that he'd sat for hours trying to take it all in. He was happy now that he could show it to Kate.

They turned in unison, hearing voices approaching from behind them. It was the woman they had passed on the road, now carrying a heavy load of firewood suspended from a wooden pole across her thin shoulders. Her three small children followed dutifully. The woman stopped beside the jeep and stared down longingly at the bunch of bananas that remained on the seat, her hungry eyes fixed on the food. Kate and Peter watched while the children approached the side of the jeep and one little girl reached out for the fruit. The woman quickly grabbed the child's arm and held it back.

Kate, seeing her camera bag on the seat beside the bananas, started toward the jeep. Peter grabbed her sleeve to hold her back. He called to the Vietnamese woman, "*Di chuoi*. Take them."

The mama san let go of her child's arm. The little girl lifted the bananas from the seat. The woman smiled briefly at Peter and walked off, her children happily eating the fruit.

Kate yanked her arm from his grasp, hurrying to her camera bag, where she took out her Nikon and shot a picture of the ruined bridge.

They climbed back into the jeep and drove off toward Tam Ky.

25

As they approached Tam Ky on Highway One, the ARVN convoy they had passed earlier was just now getting under way. A huge cloud of red dust hung over the road. The trucks moved slowly and noisily in front of the jeep. "It won't be for long," Peter said. "They'll turn off in a few kilometers."

"Is that cinnamon I smell?" Kate asked.

"It's coming from the trucks."

"My God! What unit does this convoy belong to?"

"Seventeenth Division. That's their base." Peter pointed to the west, to a city of tents at the foot of the mountains. The dusty row of trucks was turning off the highway and heading toward the base.

"We were just given an important clue to the story."

"Given?" Peter asked.

"I think Buddha may have had something to do with it."

An hour later, as the sun was just beginning to duck beneath the mountains, Peter pulled the jeep up to the Chu Lai air terminal, which was nothing but a tiny tin-roofed shack at the end of an immense stretch of runway. Kate grabbed her camera bag from the floor, but instead of stepping out of the jeep she remained glued to her seat, unable to move. Her eyes welled up with tears. "You know, Peter, you have grown a lot since I've known you."

"Three days."

"I think you understand." She kissed him hurriedly before she climbed out of the jeep. "Please don't come in, Peter. I can't stand long good-byes. Just let me go."

He watched her move to the door of the shack with her determined stride. Without looking back, she opened the door and disappeared inside.

Peter sat motionless in the jeep waiting for Kate's plane, a giant C130 transport, take off for Saigon. After watching it lumber down the runway and fade into a nearly cloudless sky, he started the jeep and hurried across the base toward the NCO Club on the beach to get drunk. Checking his .45 pistol at the door, he bought himself a pitcher of beer at the bar, received a pocketful of quarters as change, and sat down alone at a table beside the jukebox. There were already a dozen songs in line before his, mostly Chuck Berry and the Temptations—happy songs. He spent his quarters on Otis Redding's "My Girl" and Smokey Robinson's "Tracks of My Tears," the sad songs that would make him think of Kate. Never in his life had Peter felt so raw and open and exposed to the world and all the fucked-up people in it. At first he wanted to be alone with his thoughts, but three air force mechanics in need of a place to sit joined him at the table. He was actually thankful for the company—anything that would help him forget. The four of them closed the club at 4 A.M.

After they were kicked out, Peter walked down to the beach where he stumbled, with great difficulty, across the sand into the water. One of the air force men told Peter, weeks later, that he had tried to convince them he was going to swim back to the States. Although Peter didn't remember any of it, the mechanics swam out into the waves after him and dragged him back to the shore where they left him puking in the sand.

26

Peter leaned forward on Gisella's couch with his elbows on his knees and his head in his hands, staring at the floor. Peter hadn't heard her call his name. He sometimes had difficulty surfacing from the depths of the silence that easily enveloped him. He would be lost there, in the quiet, as if he were trapped beneath a huge and heavy body of water. He pictured himself lying on his back on the smooth white sand on the bottom of the sea, feeling the weight of the water press down against his chest.

"Gisella, I had a dream." She didn't acknowledge him at first. She was distracted for some reason. "Should I go on?" he asked.

"Please."

"I'd been following Kate through the back alleys of Saigon. It was like a chase scene in a movie where I could never catch up to her. I was running as fast as I could and I'd grab for her shirt and a piece would rip off in my fingers but when I'd look down at my hand the fabric would dematerialize like it had been dipped in acid. The dream was so real. I could even smell the *nuoc mam*—the smell of rotten fish. Pretty soon I'd pulled off all of Kate's clothes, piece by piece, until she was running completely naked down a long alleyway. I was barefoot. I was naked too, come to think of it. Kate would look back over her shoulder every few seconds and smile this evil sort of smile—it was eerie. Then she'd keep running.

"I had periods of telescoping vision where my eyes would be right up next to her skin until I would be so close that I could see her muscles moving just under the skin. I had this incredible sense of the structure and motion of her body as she ran. I could see even the tiny hairs on her skin. I saw beads of sweat running down her back getting caught on the hairs and then flying off in the wind. Ahhh, it was so real!"

Peter was overcome with the dream. He needed just to sit for a while.

Gisella uncrossed her legs. He became aware that he was sweating. He reached for a tissue from the box on the table and wiped off his forehead.

"Is it time to stop?"

"You've only been here for fifteen minutes."

"It seemed like I was talking for an hour at least."

"You want to continue? Is there more about your dream?"

"I think so . . . well, yes. It's slightly . . . very bizarre."

"Remember what I told you in our very first session?"

She raised her eyebrows when he looked over at her.

"Then, go on."

"I was chasing her. Finally she ran through this doorway. There was no door—only a curtain—just off the alley. Inside was a bar with a bunch of Vietnamese girls hanging around, all wearing black pajamas, only their shirts were opened so you could see their breasts. Kate was not among them when I first ran in. The mama san who worked behind the bar poured me a beer and then all the girls gathered around. They pawed me as though I was a piece of meat or something. I was sweating. It was very hot and clammy in there—very smelly too.

"I looked toward the back of the room and Kate came through another curtain. As she did, a cold blast of air came into the room—also the smell of jasmine—that beautiful sweet smell that comes from the flowers at night. Kate was dressed like an angel. She had a wreath of white flowers around her head. She was very beautiful with her dark hair and suntanned skin and the white flowers—she wore an almost invisible white gown with a necklace of flowers. Also she had a beautiful crystal hanging on a gold chain. Then she talked to me . . .

"'It's time we knew each other better,' she said. She smiled at me, her big emerald-green eyes sparkling. 'We knew one another's bodies but not enough about each other's souls,' she told me."

Peter looked up at Gisella. He could see that Gisella was quite intrigued by the dream. For a moment, that brought him out of it.

"Then?" she asked, to get him back into it.

"Kate came over and kissed me softly. That's when I knew she was an angel. But I could feel her lips on mine. She was there. She sat down on the stool next to mine at the bar. I was going to ask, *Can I buy you a drink?* but it seemed too ridiculous.

"'I don't drink.' She read my mind. 'My body's on another plane now. I don't need food or drink to survive. My new body is made of ether.'

"'Ether?' I asked."

"'It's similar to air but finer.'"

Peter stopped. That was the end of the dream. He wanted to change the subject immediately. It was too frightening being back there—wherever that was.

He felt Gisella's eyes focused on the top of his head. As he spoke, his words were filtered through his hand across his mouth. He knew it was going to be difficult for Gisella to understand. "Nina is always telling me I don't *feel*—that I'm shut off. You know what I think?" He raised up his head just enough to take a quick glimpse at Gisella. "It doesn't matter what I think . . ."

"It matters."

He was surprised she had heard his words. He had mumbled them softly, not sure he even wanted to say them.

Peter continued. "How much can you think about a fucked-up war?"

"As much as you need to."

"How much do I need to? When I've thought enough, will things get

better? I mean—shit, I can't not think about it . . ." He lifted his head.
He wanted to smile at her. ". . . That's one thing that's for sure."

They were both silent, and then when it seemed right, when enough
time had slipped like water down a stream, Gisella spoke so softly Peter
didn't hear her words at first.

"This Colonel Broward—he seems fairly horrible."

"Who?"

"Colonel Broward—can you tell me about him?"

"The personification of evil in human form. The more I met up with
him, the more I hated him." He looked over at Gisella, once again fully
aware that she was in the room.

When she saw him surface, she smiled. "So?"

"I can picture his face—round like a basketball—with his thick black
beard. Even though he shaved, his beard looked like it was painted over
his mouth and jowls. He had big lips, like a black guy."

"Was he black?"

"No, he was white—Caucasian—whatever you want to call it. White
trash. From the South—Alabama, I think. I'm sure he was a bigot. He
hated everything—like a fucking Nazi. He was out for himself. He was
out to . . . I don't know what the fuck Broward was out for."

"He was out to get you—wasn't he?"

"He was out to get me. He was out to get Marcus. He was the most
evil fucker you can imagine. He had a smell that made you sick. Just
being near him made me sick."

Gisella always tried to end her sessions on a high note. But this time,
realizing they had slipped well past the allotted hour, she was forced to
cut things off where they were. "Maybe we can go into this in more depth
at another time, Peter. I didn't realize it, but we're out of time."

"Maybe we don't need to go into it in more depth—ever," Peter
joked.

27

Kate and Randy Guest sat together at the Flower Bar in the "Saigon Hilton," the name given the dilapidated stucco building in the center of Saigon where most of the civilian correspondents lived. The building was a leftover relic from the French occupation and the bar was their meeting place; the place where more stories passed from mouth to ear than any other in Vietnam. When they found themselves in Saigon at the same time, which was rare, Kate and Randy shared a room in the hotel. Kate had changed out of the fatigues she had worn earlier in the day when she'd flown down from Chu Lai. She had on a loose-fitting cotton print dress that revealed her tanned breasts whenever she leaned across the bar to flick her ash in the ashtray—a motion not lost on Randy, who was much too obvious in his appreciation of Kate's beauty. Randy wore the standard uniform of civilian correspondents in tropical war zones, a tan khaki shirt with four pockets and epaulets and khaki pants. The two sat on stools made of bamboo and wicker. He was drinking Johnny Walker Black over ice and smoking Salems. She drank vodka and tonics and smoked Camels.

The bar bustled with life at the steamy hour of 8 P.M. and stories flew back and forth like bullets between the correspondents. Kate lit a fresh cigarette from Randy's lit Salem. Kate said, "General Morgan was particularly tight-lipped at lunch the other day . . . God, that seems so long ago."

"I won't ask you everything that went on in Chu Lai." Randy frowned.

"Good. Then back to Morgan . . ."

Randy cut her off. "Don't forget who Morgan is. Generals don't get to be generals by spilling their guts to reporters."

"He's hiding something."

"Don't be so naive, my dear. They're always hiding something!"

"No, something more than the usual military secrets. He was uncomfortable with me around."

"You make any man uncomfortable when you're around."

"I'm *serious*, Randy!"

"I'm dead serious—you're a knockout! I'm letting you know, in case no one's ever informed you—or in case no one's informed you recently."

"Randy, you're drunk."

"That's beside the point."

"It's my guess that General Tao, Broward, and Morgan are all up to something—together, I mean."

"Then by all means, keep digging."

"I am. Whatever it is, it's well covered."

"If anyone can unearth it, you can. But do it after Bangkok. We deserve our R&R. As your bureau chief, I hereby order you to quit work for ten days. The story will be waiting for you when you return. Real stories don't die . . ."

". . . they just fade away." She laughed.

"What do you say you and I fade away for the evening?"

"I'm not ready for bed yet, dear."

"Then I suppose you could twist my arm and UPI would pay for another vodka tonic."

Kate grabbed Randy's arm with two hands and gave him, as she did with her brother when she was a child, an Indian rope burn.

Randy turned to the pretty, young Vietnamese bartender, "Lili, vodka and tonic with a twist, for Kate. Another Johnny Black for me, love. By the way, what're you freezing for ice these days? Doesn't taste quite like water."

"Use monkey pee. Has more flavor." Lili laughed.

"Don't think she's kidding," Randy smiled at Kate. He leaned toward her, trying to plant a kiss on her lips, but Kate quickly backed off. "Make hers a double, Lili. Mine too. Hold the pee."

28

Kate hurried down a narrow alley through the teeming street life of early-morning Saigon. The sidewalks were filled with vendors selling fish, vegetables, dogs, and snakes, all the delicacies for the Vietnamese dinner table. She raced through the crowd in her long white cotton dress that starkly contrasted her deep tan. She was striking, not only because of her inherent beauty, but because she was a head taller than everyone. Though her hair was thick with the dust of the street, this somehow added an earthly quality to her beauty.

Kate was on a mission. She carried a small canvas bag over her shoulder and gripped a yellow pencil between her teeth. The pencil pushed her lips back in the corners, making her face as ugly as a pretty face can look. As she raced to her morning appointment, wearing only flimsy rubber sandals, her feet quickly became covered with the dusty grime of the Saigon streets. Her steps somehow seemed to carry the weight of the story she was writing. This was the Kate White who relished being in Vietnam, the most corrupt yet exciting place on earth in 1969. She felt the thrill that comes from believing she was about to unearth another clue.

She turned a corner and suddenly she was in a large open square in front of the South Vietnamese Army Headquarters—another leftover relic from the French. The stucco building was monumental in scale, pockmarked by bullets, and decayed by the entropy that the heat and rain of the Tropics effect on all things both animate and inanimate.

Thinking only of her interview, Kate forgot to show her press card as she hurried through the gate. Immediately, an angry ARVN guard grabbed her by the arm. Seizing the opportunity to exhibit the deep-felt animosity toward Western women that many Vietnamese men felt, he spared Kate no mercy and pushed her up against the iron gate with his highly polished M-16.

The sergeant of the guard strutted out of the small booth. He had a smirk on his face, the kind Kate wished she could've wiped off with a bullet in his forehead. Pulling the pencil from her mouth, she told him, "I'm late for an appointment with General Tao."

"The general not here," the sergeant smirked.

"Call his office." Kate spoke determinedly, even though the soldier still held his weapon against her chest. He slid the M-16 upward, pressing it hard against her throat, choking her, making it impossible for her to speak. The sergeant nodded to a guard in the booth. The soldier picked up the phone. "We call, but remember what I tell you," the sergeant said to Kate, "General Tao not here!"

Kate coughed. She spat the pencil from her mouth and pushed back at the guard's weapon with all her strength, enough to relieve the pressure on her throat. "Tell him!" she managed to squeak out.

The sergeant stepped up and put his hand on the guard's weapon, pressing it tighter against Kate's throat. "What make you think General Tao here?" he glared into her eyes. Kate, unable to move against the power of the two men, spat in the sergeant's face. He remained, outwardly, unmoved. The look of intense hate he held on his face for this brash Western woman, and all the independence she displayed, revealed what was to Kate the crux of the war. The sergeant's face revealed why the war could never be won by a Western nation, because he, this ARVN sergeant, would not let it be won.

Immediately, the sun dried the spit on his face. Without wiping it off, and with his eyes never leaving Kate's, he pressed his heavy combat boot into the top of her bare foot. He twisted the heel of his boot from side to side, relishing the expression of pain on her face. When he satisfied himself, he pulled the guard's weapon away from Kate's throat and said, "General Tao see you now."

Kate hurried through the gate toward the headquarters building, and though her foot was bleeding and the pain was excruciating, she walked without a limp. She never looked down, nor back at the guards.

29

General Tao's spacious office was nearly devoid of decoration except for an elegant Louis Quatorze desk and the ubiquitous statue of Buddha on a credenza against one wall. General Tao, as stoic as a piece of furniture himself, looked out the tall window behind his desk where he could see the front courtyard and the guard post. Escorted by the general's aide, Kate entered the office trying to hide her limp. Although her foot was bleeding she smiled, not wanting the incident at the gate to overshadow the interview. When the general heard his assistant leave and the door close, he spoke with his back still to Kate. "*Chao ong*, Kate White—hello."

"*Toi manh*," she said, "very well, thanks."

"You are brave as any man, Kate White. Your episode with the guards reveals a great deal about you."

Kate, quickly getting down to business, said, "General, you are the one to be revealed this morning."

She stood beside the general's desk. Finally he turned from the window and looked at Kate. Sensing her pain, he ran his eyes down her body to her feet where he stopped. "*Moi ong ngoi*—sit down," he told her. "We must attend to your wound."

General Tao walked effeminately across the soft carpet toward Kate as she sat down in the large chair in front of his desk. As he approached, he pulled the white silk ARVN officer's scarf from around his neck. Kneeling directly at Kate's feet, as if worshiping an idol, he removed the sandal from her wounded foot. Gently, he dressed the wound with his scarf. As he lifted her foot, holding it tenderly in his small hands, he took a simple bow forward and kissed her muddy ankle. Kate watched the top of General Tao's small head as he began to pitifully caress her calves. A pang of nausea ran up her esophagus until she tasted stomach acid in her throat. His round smooth face, the look in his eyes, his shiny wet lips, all contributed to her disgust.

The general pushed Kate's long skirt up her leg, carefully folding it over as he went, until the skirt was up to her waist and her panties were revealed. Kate, understanding this to be the price for the interview, allowed his advances. He spoke softly, heatedly as he ran his hands along her long legs. "I know what you want from me. You think everything should be revealed . . ."

"Isn't that what you want from me?"

"You and I easily cross the borders between East and West," he smiled.

"I was born in a Western country that has survived in the Orient."

"Perhaps that explains why you have survived so well in Vietnam. You know our mind"—General Tao touched Kate's panties and started to pull them down—"so you take advantage of us."

Kate lifted herself off the chair for a moment to allow her panties to slip off. "The advantage is always yours, General Tao." He slid her panties down to her ankles, his eyes never diverting for even a second from the sight of Kate's vagina. "As a woman, you are taking advantage of me, as a man."

Tao pulled Kate's panties gingerly over her feet and, still on his knees, spread her thighs farther and continued to look unabashedly between her legs. A bubble of saliva formed in the corner of his mouth as he spoke. "It is your openness I admire. Vietnamese women are so much more closed. Our women are slaves to the men, taught to serve, not to think or speak. Not like you, Kate White—you say whatever you like."

He laughed, and as he did he slid his palm along Kate's soft inner thigh until the tips of his thin manicured fingers touched the lips of Kate's open, pink vagina.

Abruptly, unexpectedly, Tao stood. He suddenly became a general again and walked around behind his big general's desk. Kate's panties were left on the floor. When Tao spoke again, his voice was deeper, harsher, back to business. "But now you must go, Miss White."

"But you haven't . . ."

"But I have. The interview is finished." Angrily, he slammed his fist down on the desk. "You must leave! *Tien! Tien!*"

Kate stood up in front of her chair. She bent down to pick up her panties from the floor but did not do what the general expected. She did not put them back on or in her pocket or throw them at him in anger; she simply folded them neatly, placing them in front of the general on his desk, and said, "A gift from the reporter who will expose you."

30

Kate wanted nothing more than to get back to the hotel, to a hot bath. She felt dirty and used, although this wasn't the first time she'd felt this way since she'd arrived in Vietnam three years ago. When she considered why she was there in the first place, or why she had stayed for so long, or why she didn't leave—her thinking always turned back to the job. She had won her job with UPI after seven hard years during and after college with the *Sydney Times*. Being able to work with Randall Guest was an honor—God, so many people had told her that, that she was now fully convinced it was true. Their relationship was more father-daughter than that of lovers. Although they shared an apartment—a large room really, in the Saigon Hilton—they hadn't slept together for two years. Randy was not attractive to her, and really had never been—too big, too sweaty—he smelled like raw meat, she had thought. Many correspondents felt Randall Guest was the best in the business, certainly one of the best newsmen in Vietnam. So Kate felt obligated to feel grateful for the way he had taken her under his wing. She had learned more about writing and how to follow a story than in all her years in Sydney. In a weird way she did love him, she thought.

It was with these thoughts running through her mind when a young Vietnamese boy on a bicycle nearly crashed into her on the way back to the hotel. He swerved to miss her and fell off his bike onto the hot pavement. Immediately, Kate bent down to help him. He seemed to have hurt his arm. But the boy began to yell obscenities at her in English. "Fucking bitch! Fucking cunt! Why you no watch where you walk!"

Stunned, Kate backed off quickly, scurrying away, losing herself, as she had done a million times, swallowed up inside the throngs of Vietnamese crowding the street. She asked herself again why she remained in this country where hate bubbled up so easily from where it lay, just beneath the surface. Though she didn't want to think of him at all, thoughts of Peter flashed through her mind. He brought out a much-too-vulnerable side of her. She felt that with him she could actually dare to open her heart a little. With the other men she'd met in Nam—with all of them—she merely did business. Even the ones she'd slept with; she could rationalize that it was always for business reasons—part of what Randy had taught her to do, which meant doing *whatever it takes.*

Again, Kate was thinking of Peter as she passed a woman selling some jewelry spread out on a small square of black silk on the sidewalk. She stopped for a moment with the thought of buying him a ring. Rolling the ring between her thumb and index finger, if for only a moment, made her feel a chink in her armor. Again, her protective voice told her to put the ring back down on the silk. No, she agreed with the voice, she didn't want to encourage his feelings for her. It wasn't fair to him. But as she stood up again, with the Vietnamese woman's sad eyes following her, Kate admitted to herself for the first time that she might actually be in love. "Oh God, I can't do that!" she heard the voice telling her again that he was too young, too inexperienced. It was as if she was being given a way out.

As she wove her way between the Vietnamese women and children crowding the street, her mind seemed to keep up with the motion of her body no matter how fast she walked. The voice told her that she was not going to allow herself to fall in love with a soldier. Then it told her she couldn't bear the loss if he was killed. But beneath all these words was the truth, which was simply the feeling she had when she was with him, including the feeling she had when he looked at her, whenever he ran his fingers across her skin, whenever they kissed.

An American military policeman held open the hotel door for Kate. "Morning, ma'am." He flashed a smile as she sped past.

"Thank you, Private." She returned his smile. Something about the soldier reminded her of Peter. She thought it might be his innocent demeanor. They seemed about the same age, nineteen, but a *young* nineteen. It wasn't just that—it was something else—could it be innocence? He wasn't yet jaded, wasn't yet closed off. So yes, that must be it—innocence—another reason, and a very good one, why she could not allow herself to fall.

At the top of the stairs, Kate aimed her well-worn key toward the door lock. Before she could turn it, the door opened and there was Randy, freshly shaven and cleanly dressed, heading out to the bureau a few blocks from the hotel.

"Oh, hello, love. I thought you'd be going back to the bureau after your interview."

"I need a bath, Randy. I need to wash Tao off my skin."

"My God—you slept with him?"

"God, Randy! That is not going to happen with Tao—not unless he turns over his Swiss bank account to me. No, my need is psychological, but I still need to wash him off me."

"Yes, he is fairly slimy." Randall pecked Kate on the cheek as he slipped his big frame out the doorway. "So, you'll fill me in then after your bath."

"Yes, I'll be down in a while."

Randy locked the door from the outside, knowing that Kate wouldn't bother to lock herself in. This annoyed him because Saigon was no place, even in their hotel where MPs stood guard on the sidewalk, not to lock a door. Caucasian women were raped by soldiers all the time.

Kate rushed into the bedroom, throwing her small canvas bag on the chair by the window. She walked over to the antique desk sitting against the adjoining wall, where she pulled a teak jewelry case with her store of marijuana from the top drawer. The box contained two packs of prerolled joints disguised as Winston cigarettes complete with filters in addition to a small tin of opium. She lit a joint, taking two long hits of the potent Thai grass—anxious to forget her meeting with General Tao.

She walked to the window where she leaned her back against the frame waiting for the marijuana to take effect. Kate stood looking down at the street slowly unbuttoning her cotton dress, letting it fall to the floor. She watched Randy cross to the sidewalk on the other side, dapper in his starched khaki shirt and trousers. As he disappeared around the corner, she remained standing by the open window. She stood behind the weightless sheer curtain, which was all that separated her naked body from the eyes of the Vietnamese office workers in the building across the street. She thought of Peter again, and as she did she dropped her head, noticing the way the curtain had wrapped itself around her legs. She pulled the shear fabric slightly to the side, letting it slide off her leg, seeing how it made her look as if she was standing in a long evening gown—her bare skin exposed up to the hip. She let her hand fall between her legs where her fingers ran across the soft hair on her vagina. Her eyes closed and she dreamed again of the young sol-dier she'd left in Chu Lai.

Kate loved the bathroom in their apartment, which was built during the height of the French occupation of Vietnam, when the spice barons and the rubber barons came to visit their plantations in this place they called "Indochine." She imagined Saigon was even more decadent then—the steamy streets teeming with French soldiers who smoked Gauloises and Gitanes and had a fondness for absinthe. The bathroom walls were tiled in huge squares of white, with stripes of ultramarine blue running in a ribbon all the way around the room. Reaching the bathroom door, they went up and over the top—a luxury from a time when craftsmanship was still highly prized.

Everything was oversized. The old French toilet, made of bright white porcelain, was big enough to fall into. Kate had once walked in on the Vietnamese maid taking a pee. The girl, who was probably only four feet ten or eleven inches, stood squatting on the seat, having to spread her legs uncomfortably far apart. The bidet was the same size. But it was the tub that was Kate's place of refuge. It took half an hour just to fill it—its length being about six feet, its breadth and depth about four. The hotel water ran slowly from the tap and was of indeterminate temperature, changing from scalding hot to room temperature in seconds, so that the tub when filled to the top was almost always a rather pleasant warm temperature, perfect for a long soak in a tropical climate.

Kate paced around the bathroom impatient as the water poured slowly from the brass spigot. The water had turned an amber tint about halfway through the filling, from the accumulation of rust in the ancient plumbing. Secretly, she rather liked the color. It didn't bother her as it did Randy, who threw a fit whenever it happened. "This goddamn shithole of a country can't even provide clean water—even the water turns the color of shit!"

Watching herself in the four-foot mirror behind the sink, Kate turned her body to the side, measuring with her eyes the flatness of her stomach that had always remained slim and tight. Sliding her palms up over her ribs, she pushed up her breasts to assure herself of their firmness. Not overly large, she felt their size matched her body perfectly. She pulled her shoulders back, pushing them out as far as they would go. Peter had told her how beautiful her breasts were. Then he had circled her nipples with his tongue, a motion she felt had been quite sophisticated for a nineteen-year-old. She heard the water spill over onto the bathroom floor and as she spun around to turn off the tub faucet, she checked out her ass in the mirror. Her best attribute, she bragged to herself, silently. She turned back to have another look in the mirror after turning off the water. Standing for a moment longer than she usually would, she ran her eyes down her body, along her legs to the floor, and back up again. Her eyes passed over the makeup kit on the sink. She looked up at her face in the mirror, at her eyes in particular. She leaned close to the mirror fumbling inside the makeup kit for an eyebrow pencil. Feeling the cold porcelain sink against her thighs, she brought the pencil to her face, drawing a black line along the edge of her right eyebrow. At the side, instead of stopping, she elongated the line. Then she drew another line along the underside of her eye carefully joining it with the top one at both ends. She repeated this with her left eye until she was satisfied with her work. Stepping back, she smiled into the mirror appreciating the transformation. A cloud of steam rising up from the surface of the hot water gathered around her body while she continued to gaze into the almond-shaped eyes in the mirror.

When Kate stepped into the tub, the water cascaded over the edge onto the bathroom floor. Holding her breath, she dunked underwater, thinking of the young soldier who had not been at all shy about kissing her from head to toe.

She opened her eyes underwater. The tropical light filtered through the bathroom shutters, creating stripes that wrapped themselves around the curves of her body—an effect that seemed to heighten the otherworldliness of Vietnam. Kate's mind became lost within a dream of the beauty of her own body. She knew what it was that men saw in her. She saw it herself—the shape of her long legs, her firm stomach, the way her thigh muscle tightened when she lifted her leg up to the edge of the tub. Even her feet and her toes were pretty, which is why she almost always wore sandals.

When she came up for air, Kate was in such a hurry to dunk back under that she took a breath too soon and swallowed some water. She coughed, which broke the spell she was in. When she stopped she quickly gulped a deep breath of air, sliding once again into the womb of the warm liquid, the place where she felt so totally alone and safe in the world.

While Kate was still underwater, the hotel maid, a young Vietnamese girl about sixteen, walked into the bathroom with a bucket of cleaning utensils. A moment after the girl had started scrubbing the sink, Kate burst up out of the water again, gasping loudly for air. The girl, who had thought the bathroom was empty and was standing with her back to the tub, let out a frightful scream and ran out of the apartment.

31

Peter was sound asleep when Marcus woke him by slamming the screen door to the PIO hootch. "Get up. We've got orders for a fucking top-secret mission." Even before he fully was awake, something didn't feel right to Peter.

"*Whose* orders, Marcus? How come they didn't come through the PIO?"

"Because they ain't *from* the PIO." Marcus was unusually annoyed for the most laid-back guy Peter had ever known.

"Where are they fucking from then?"

"A LRRP."

"A fucking LRRP?"

LRRP stood for Long Range Reconnaissance Platoon, the name given the soldiers whose missions included kidnapping NVA officers from their headquarters. Peter didn't like the sound of what Marcus was telling him. Usually their orders came directly from Major Pinkham back in Chu Lai, the officer in charge of the Americal Division PIO. But as combat photographers, they were eligible to work for anybody who needed photographs. Sometimes, orders would come directly from the commanding officer of a company who needed the use of a combat correspondent—when the company had found a large NVA encampment or weapons cache or something that warranted a story or photographs.

Marcus had been told nothing about the mission other than they'd
be photographing something far into the jungle—perhaps even near the
border of Laos.

"Something about this is fucked up."

"Look." Marcus frowned, growing pissed. "This captain comes up to
me in the mess tent—I don't even know how he even fucking knew my
name, but he did. And he says to go get you and we're both to report to
the LRRP chopper pad at oh six hundred. It's five fucking forty-five right
now, so get your shit together. I don't want to fuck with that bastard—
he's like Broward all over again."

"This sounds like something Broward's cooked up," Peter said.

"We're supposed to meet this LRRP, Staff Sergeant Avery, at the
pad," Marcus said, as Peter poured water over his head from the jerry can
by the back door. Oh six hundred was the usual time for the first chopper out.

They both knew who Avery was. He was one of the LRRPs everyone
knew—together with a guy they called "Governor," a Brit who'd been a
mercenary in the Middle East. Peter and Marcus had done a story about
the LRRPs so they knew something of what went on with them. One
thing they had learned was that LRRP missions always seemed to be covered by a cloud of secrecy. When the two reporters had been working on
their story, the LRRPs fed them only scraps about their mission—never
revealing the whole truth. At times, Peter and Marcus felt they were
being lied to. Maybe that was part of the LRRP modus operandi as well.
They acted in small teams, eight or less—sometimes only one or two. To
maintain secrecy, they followed their own private chain of command.
They often dressed as Vietnamese, wearing black pajamas and carrying
AK-47s. They infiltrated enemy camps and captured North Vietnamese
officers, sometimes torturing them to extract information—"heavy shit,"
as Marcus would say.

Whatever it was that Marcus and Peter didn't yet know about this
mission, it already seemed to have a bad feeling. In Vietnam everyone
learned to trust *having a bad feeling*. The sporadic weapons fire they heard

as they headed down to the chopper pad sounded like nothing more than popcorn popping compared to what Peter imagined they were in for.

The chopper pad the LRRPs used on the north side of LZ Danger was the one used mostly for resupply of equipment and ammunition. It was where the huge Sikorsky Sky Hooks dropped down the giant metal tanks filled with drinking water. This was not the usual chopper pad for slicks and, for that reason alone, Peter had the uneasy feeling that their mission was likely to be jinxed. Vietnam brought out the worst of everyone's superstitious nature. Something as simple as a mission beginning from the wrong place could jinx it. But more than that, this one had a certain strange flavor all its own. It felt even stranger as they arrived at the pad just as the sun was coming up. The place, together with the men, seemed vague and unfamiliar—the men seemed to be part of another army involved in some sort of underground war.

There were several small groups of LRRPs scattered around the perimeter of the supply pad. The pad itself was made up of mats of woven metal linked together into a square big enough for a helicopter to land on. As they stepped across looking for the group they were to link up with, they could feel yesterday's heat radiating up from the metal. At first Peter didn't recognize Avery when he'd come up from behind and tapped him on the shoulder. Peter didn't recall Avery had worn a mustache.

"Hill?"

"Yes."

"Zablinsky?"

"Zabriski," Peter corrected him.

"Yer in the right place."

"Where're we going?" Marcus asked.

"You'll find out later." Peter didn't like the sound of that. "You bring plenty of film?"

"Twenty rolls—ten each." Peter tugged at the two bulging pockets on his chest.

Avery nodded. Peter could see his piercing blue eyes were checking him out, icily. He figured Avery was deciding how much he was going to tell them about the mission. Peter thought also—and he was sure he was right about this—that Avery was checking to see what kind of soldiers he and Marcus were. Could they be trusted when the going got tough? "We'll be flying out to a base camp about forty klicks west of here" is all that seemed necessary for Avery to say.

Peter didn't ask him anything more. For one thing, he wasn't even sure the information Avery had fed him was true or not. He figured Avery would tell them only what he wanted them to hear and that maybe it was even misinformation.

Avery asked if they'd left their dog tags and wallets behind. Peter assured him they had. It gave him the creeps to head out to the field without his wallet, which was, after all, the place he kept his amulets and good-luck charms. He had the feeling he might not survive this mission without it.

Marcus and Peter tried to make themselves comfortable on some sandbags, leaning against each other's backs. Marcus pulled a comic from his pocket. Peter pulled his bush hat down over his eyes and tried to sleep. It was about two hours later and twenty degrees hotter when their chopper finally arrived. It wasn't until then that they knew which members of the LRRPs were the ones picked for their mission. Avery stood in the prop wash holding his black beret down on his head when three others got up off the hot sheets of metal, their sawed-off carbines in hand, and silently climbed into the chopper.

There they were again—spying the war from ten thousand feet above the jungle floor where Vietnam became just a sea of mountains of green, one more beautiful than the next. So incongruous, Peter thought, that a country where the mountains had the power to take your breath away could be the most evil place on the face of the earth. Flying west, the bright, iridescent green of the rice paddies gave way to the darker, richer color of the highland grasses. The ridges of the hills ran east–west, with the narrow valleys dark and hidden slits between them. They passed over some abandoned LZs, which from that altitude looked like nothing more than tiny shaved-off mountaintops on their way to becoming reclaimed by the jungle. After those, there were no more signs of life at all. Just bomb craters turned into ponds filled by the heavy monsoon rains. The last sign of human meddling was a huge mountain that had been defoliated by what surely must have been re-lentless bombing. It had been NVA headquarters for this part of South Vietnam and had also housed a huge hospital, all hidden underground. From the air, the entrances to the tunnels made the mountain look like a huge chunk of Swiss cheese. *Really* eerie. After that, there was noth-ing but jungle. Jungle so deep it looked like you could press your finger into it and your finger would just keep sinking deeper—like it would turn into something soft and squishy like pudding.

The mission was supposed to last only one or two days, max. And since they were going to be humping a great distance through some very inhospitable terrain, they carried no packs—it was necessary to travel light. Canteens of water, bandoleers of ammunition, and food stuffed in their pant pockets were all the things they carried. Specifically, four cans of C rats, two LRRP rations, and two two-quart canteens. Peter forgot his insect repellent but Marcus brought some. His machete hung from his web belt. Peter left his .45 back in the hootch because it was too heavy. Marcus and Peter had each brought ten rolls of army-issue DuPont black-and-white film and their cameras. The squad had no ponchos, no poncho liners to sleep on, no entrenching tools, no C-4 explosive, no machine gun, no grenade launcher. It was so hot they wore only shirts, pants, and bush hats—no helmets or flak jackets.

The secrecy that surrounded this mission seemed odd. Comparing it to what they'd witnessed already in their six months as combat cor-respondents, it qualified to be near the top of the list of what was fucked up about being in Nam. So much of this mystery called the Vietnam War, which was continually unfolding like a surrealistic novel, was odd that it was sometimes difficult to tell the difference between what was and what was not odd. A tiger with three heads—that might have qualified as odd.

Peter's heart pounded in his chest when the Huey began its descent. There had been no signs of a village nearby. Judging from the length of the flight, it seemed they were even farther into the bush than Avery had let on.

The temporary laager where the chopper dropped the small squad of men was creepy with a large C—*Creepy.* The chopper skimmed above the treetops for a few kilometers before it suddenly dropped down into the center of a small meadow. As they landed, Peter looked out at the protective perimeter where soldiers sat with M-16s or M-60 machine guns facing into the tree line. That didn't seem unusual, just a routine precaution for any slick bringing in food or ammo. And the door gunners on the chopper didn't seem more cautious than normal. But still, there was something that made Peter queasy, something he couldn't quite put his finger on.

One of the little things that didn't figure was the uncommon polite-ness of the guys there. It seemed like they knew something he didn't— and they weren't going to tell him. The grunts went about their business with smiles on their faces—fake smiles.

The laager wasn't that unusual physically. It was a platoon-sized camp with shallow foxholes dug around the perimeter, the better ones covered with banana leaves laid over sticks of bamboo. Within the camp, twenty or so GIs sat cleaning their weapons, cooking their beanie wee-nies in cans held over glowing blue heat tabs or small chunks of C-4 ex-plosive.

Avery was summoned to meet the commanding officer, a LRRP cap-tain. The two of them spent thirty minutes huddled over a map before Avery returned to clue the men in. Though they were already more than seventy kilometers west of civilization, deeper into the boonies than any of them had ever been, Avery reported they would be humping quite a bit farther. The captain came over to offer them food, which had been flown out on the chopper with them. It wasn't C rations, but a specially prepared meal of spaghetti and fresh-baked bread and iced tea. While they ate, Avery unfolded the map, setting it on the ground in the middle of the small circle of six. He ran his finger alongside a small stream, which snaked its way up a valley and into the mountains. He pointed out their present location for the first time, which showed how far west they had already come. But Avery remained vague about the purpose of the mission. He called the destination "a ridgeline," but that was all he would say. Peter could tell, even from a cursory look, that the marching, what they called humping, was going to be tough. What he saw on the map— what they all saw—were the mountains becoming steeper and taller, the valleys deeper, and the vegetation thicker. It was where Charlie loved to hide. The main supply lines of the North Vietnamese were along these valleys. These were the trails they used to carry in rockets for shelling the big American bases along the seacoast. They would truck them down from North Vietnam through Laos along the Ho Chi Minh Trail and then head east on foot, carrying the heavy rockets on their shoulders toward the coast where almost all the big American bases were situated. In these valleys grew some of the thickest jungles on earth. It wasn't easy going for Charlie—and wouldn't be for Avery's group.

Because these routes were well traveled, it was more than likely they would run into Charlie along the way. Peter began every mission searching for Charlie behind every tree and every rock until somewhere along the way, he'd just grow tired and stop looking.

32

It was hot, maybe 105 degrees. In the order they humped in, walking point was an Indian, a scout named Catchahorse, nicknamed Kemosabee. Then came Dan Sullivan, a quiet Irish guy with red hair and freckles. Then Marcus and Peter. Behind them was a tall and skinny kid who looked about fifteen, named Spellbinder, who looked like he could have been a real fuck-up except that he was a LRRP. Then finally came Avery who always had a serious look on his face, which fit his reputation for being tough as nails. The way Avery carried his sawed-off carbine across his stomach made him look like he could win the war all alone if he had enough ammunition. Peter thought that, with his new mustache, he looked like Pancho Villa who had gotten lost and was fighting in the wrong country.

"Saddle up, girls," said Avery, with an uncharacteristic smile on his face, his way of saying, *We're all in this together.*

Almost immediately after leaving the camp they ran into the stream they would be following for the entire journey. Its quick curves forced them to cross back and forth frequently in order to maintain a fairly straight line. The water was cold and unusually clear. It was deep enough so that the canteens around their waists helped float them across. Peter and Marcus held both their weapons and their cameras above their heads to keep them dry. Peter used a small tree trunk to pull himself up the embankment on the other side. Then he turned around, offering his weapon for Marcus to grab on to.

"Don't shoot," Marcus joked, "I'm gonna die fucking soon enough."

"Don't even say that. I'd be lost in this shithole without you, man!"

"I just saved your ass from a six-inch water leech. He was trackin' you—about to stick his ugly self on your back."

"I owe you one."

"You owe me a fucking million, man."

They all saw Avery pause in the stream, looking intently down into the clear water. His hand shot down into the water and, with a smile flashing on his face, pulled out a giant leech. He refused a hand up the bank offered by Peter. Instead, he climbed up himself, holding the leech above his head like a trophy. He set it on the ground and chopped it to pieces with his survival knife.

"Your lunch, Avery?" Marcus joked.

"I'm preparing it for you, motherfuck." He held up a slice, impaled on the point of his knife blade. "Care for a bite?" he asked, looking at Marcus. Instead, placing it carefully between his teeth, he ate it himself. "Mmmh, tasty."

Avery had made his point showing everyone who was the baddest motherfucker on the block. He returned his knife to its sheath and pulled a folded map from his shirt pocket. "Let's have a look, while Zabriski's enjoying lunch," he joked.

All the members of the patrol huddled around the map. Avery's gnarled index finger again followed the imaginary line into the dense jungle. Spellbinder exclaimed, "Hey, that's Laos!" He pointed to the border, which followed the mountain range from north to south.

"No shit, Sherlock!" said Avery, crossing his eyes for effect right in Spellbinder's face.

"We're not at war with Laos. We can't go there."

"No shit—we *ain't* there. If we get captured, the army never knew us."

The word *captured* rattled through everyone's brain.

"Gee," Marcus joked, "sounds like a great way to spend an afternoon."

"Finish yer lunch now, Zabriski, or you won't get dessert," Avery scowled back.

"What's for dessert, Mom?"

"Fried asshole—yers!"

"So this is Broward's idea. Send us into fucking Laos to get captured by the North fucking Vietnamese and we can't even admit we had orders to go."

Zabriski added, "Ain't Broward a fuck."

Avery got serious, "You wanna bullshit, or you wanna hear our mission?"

Private Spellbinder lit up a smoke.

"Anyone who wants a smoke better do it now," Avery grumbled. "Ain't gonna be no fuckin' smoke between here and the trail."

"The trail? What trail?" Danny Sullivan asked.

"The one named after Ho Chi Minh, fucknuts," said Avery.

"We're humpin' the fuckin' Ho Chi Minh fuckin' Trail?" Marcus exclaimed. "Nobody humps the Ho Chi Minh 'cept the North Vietnamese! Are you fuckin' crazy, Avery?"

"Yeah, and yer goin' with me."

Sullivan asked, "So what're we supposed to do when we get there?"

Marcus answered, "Fight the whole North Vietnamese Army, right? The six of us! Somehow I know Broward's behind this . . . the motherfucker really wants our asses in a sling."

"What if we just don't go?" asked Spellbinder. "*I'm* for not going."

Avery said, "You don't follow orders, you get court-martialed, like anybody that don't follow orders. But you'll never make it to your court-martial, 'cuz I'll shoot you first!" After that, Spellbinder kept his mouth shut. "Zabriski and Hill are gonna photograph the movement on the trail. Those are their orders. Now they know what they gotta do. The rest of us—we're goin' along for the ride."

Marcus and Peter looked at each other. The look said it all.

Marcus shook his head, "Fuckin' Laos! That's Uncle Sam—always fuckin' where he shouldn't."

"You wanna make a political speech, Zabriski? You runnin' for senator?" Avery smirked.

"Impressive, Avery! Didn't think you ever heard of Congress."

Avery grabbed Marcus's shirt. Peter pulled Avery's hand off him.

"Owe you one," Marcus smiled.

"No—I owe you one less," Peter said.

Avery looked up at Catchahorse. "Whaddya think, Kemosabee—this the best route up to the trail?" He pointed with that finger of his, which, like all his fingers, had no nail left.

"No," answered Catchahorse, "better follow the stream."

Avery asked why.

"Just a guess."

"We'll check it out when we get there. You'll check it out, Kemosabee."

Getting back to business, Avery said, "Saddle up, girls. This is some beaucoup bad country we're runnin' into—an' I don't just mean Charlie. I'm talkin' cobras, vipers, leeches—shit like that."

"Shit, Catchahorse eats viper for breakfast," Sullivan said.

Marcus who was still pissed, looked at Avery. "Avery eats anything. I heard you eat your mother for dinner—in front of the TV."

The farther west they humped the more strange the jungle became. Everything seemed to have grown weirdly out of human proportion. The squad, like miniature toy soldiers, continued following the stream as it snaked through elephant grass twenty feet tall. They took great care stepping between the towering blades, which were so sharp they'd easily cut through the skin. The jungle seemed odd, even for Vietnam.

When they finally emerged from the elephant grass, they found themselves for the first time on top of an embankment about fifteen meters above the stream. Each of the men in turn slid down the slippery bank, splashing back into the cool water. Catchahorse waited on the bank across the river and extended his hand to pull each man up the other side. He was a lot stronger than his small frame let on.

The squad continued along the left side of the stream as it slithered in ever-faster curves, making its way down from the mountains looming above them. They entered a plateau of low grass springing out of the mud like hairs from a scalp—a kind of savanna where the ground became soft. The savanna turned out to be almost a hundred meters across although it took nearly an hour to cross. Everyone was silently angry that Catchahorse had led them in that direction. They knew that if Charlie had caught them there, they were dead meat—their feet were glued to the ground. Maybe Catchahorse saw no other choice. It was true that the jungle across the stream looked too thick to move through. It looked like a tall and impenetrable green hedge.

As Peter thought of it, the brand of mud used to build Vietnam was of the finest grade—so refined that running it between thumb and index finger there was no graininess whatsoever. Extremely high in clay content, the mud would bake almost to the consistency of pottery when the rains stopped and the 110-degree sun beat down upon it. But when it was wet, it would grab around a foot and leg, holding it in place in its death grip. The more a man struggled, the more the mud held fast. When he finally managed, gathering all his strength, to pull a foot out, swearing to himself he'd never go through that again—he'd be forced to, with his next step.

The men were happy when they had finally crossed the savanna and returned to the river, where they used the water to wash the mud off their boots and pant legs. It was then that they began to feel a cold damp air against their skin. A klick past the savanna, the land gently started to rise up into what was the side of the mountain they were about to climb. Their route took them along a ridge made up of a series of bumps, each about ten meters high, which Peter imagined as a spine of a dog. He pictured huge boulders beneath the ground as the vertebrae.

Then came the mountain. The ground was covered with vines con-
necting like endless strips of Velcro with one intertwined so tightly with
the next that the only way through was to chop their way with machetes.
The vegetation was resilient and fibrous and had to be held with one
hand and chopped cleanly with the other. Because the mountain was so
steep, the process was tiring for the men, who were forced to hold the
heavy machetes above their heads. Meanwhile the ground underfoot,
covered with wet leaves, was as slippery as ice.

Catchahorse passed back the word to watch for green bamboo vipers
clinging to the vines. It was nearly impossible to tell the snakes from the
vines since they were identical in circumference and color. The only visible difference was that the snakes had eyes.

The higher they climbed, the darker it became beneath the tree
cover. The three canopies above them, which allowed the sun to shine
only through small slits between the leaves, served to thin the vegetation and make moving easier. The feeling was one of being a speck on
the floor of a hideously gigantic room. It was as if they had entered a
huge dark cathedral with cold and damp walls. The tree trunks grew
mostly a meter or two in diameter. The leaves were a foot long. Even
the boulders, washed clean by the stream, were of gigantic proportion—big round ominous balls five or seven meters or more across and
slippery with moss. The smell of the mold was overpowering. It hurt
the lungs to breathe. Everywhere were signs of decay. It was as if this
was the place where the world decomposed.

As they fought their way up, the loose earth slipped away under their
feet. Since there was little hope of getting a foothold on the loose ground
beside the stream, it was easier to climb straight up the sheer rock faces
in the stream even with the water cascading down on top of them.

They stopped to drink at a pool carved smoothly into a rock by a wa-
terfall. While the men filled their canteens, Avery took the opportunity to show them their exact position on the map. The six of them
huddled around Avery, silently shivering in their soaked fatigues, their

eyes following while the familiar index finger again traced a line from the laager, now about twenty-five klicks behind, to their destination. Seeing how far they were from the relative safety and protection of support troops, and how far they were from artillery range, gave them the inexorable feeling of having been abandoned, not only by their country, but by the army as well.

Their route had not been marked on the map should it, along with their unmarked bodies, fall into Charlie's hands. If they were captured, they would look like six little lambs who'd simply lost their way—lambs who had somehow stumbled up a sheer mountain ridge that, as it happened, was the ridge that for hundreds of years had separated South Vietnam from Laos.

The place was far off the eerie scale. Eerie enough so that nobody, except Avery, spoke at all. It turned out that the pool where they stopped was just below their destination. He simply pointed straight up with five pairs of eyes following his finger. There was a spider's web just above their heads stretching between the trees. The size of the web made each of the men wonder just how big a spider it would take to fashion such a monstrous thing. It seemed her body would have to be the size of a tennis ball.

As steep as the next part of the climb was, the thought of climbing was less painful than the thought of sitting on the rocks beneath the gigantic spider's web. The sheer wall they faced would have been, under normal circumstances, a technical climb that demanded ropes, pitons, and carabiners, none of which they carried. Instead, they were forced to construct a human ladder to make it to the top.

When they started up again, each of them made sure not to disturb the sleeping giant that none of them wanted to meet. Catchahorse was the only one who saw the spider. He watched her scurry up a tree, her foot-long legs gripping easily around the trunk.

33

It was afternoon by the time they reached the edge of the cliff. With what felt like his last ounce of strength, Peter pulled his chin up over the edge. There was no trail in sight. The only thing he saw was leaves. No open space at all. Instead, there was brush so thick it was impossible to see more than a foot in front of his face. The squad huddled close. Avery held his finger across his lips and the men listened to Vietnamese voices passing by only a few meters from where they sat. Every so often a truck would pass, the men listening to the sound of an engine struggling to push a heavy load. A few minutes afterward, the smell of diesel filtered through the thick growth of leaves.

Peter's vision of the Ho Chi Minh Trail had gained huge proportions during the day's journey it had taken to get there. Superhighway dimensions. He had imagined a muddy but wide-open freeway clogged with big Russian-built trucks with red stars on their doors, lumbering along one right after another. In his imagination, the trucks carried NVA soldiers in crisp new uniforms whistling patriotic songs through their betel-stained teeth. The reality turned out to be very different—they had arrived and there was nothing to see.

It was hot again where they hid. Even the ground beneath them was hot. Frozen solid in the jungle heat, they remained silent, waiting for the voices to disappear. They knew if they were discovered there was no way out except straight down the sheer cliff behind them, a cliff it had taken several hours to climb. Everyone in the squad was acutely aware of being trapped on a thin sliver of earth between the Ho Chi Minh Trail and the precipice. They had been given orders to maintain radio silence once they entered Laos. Even if they were to radio for help, nobody was going to rescue them. The army wasn't going to allow an American helicopter to fly into Laos and cause a major international incident—not on their account. And even if they did allow it, a chopper wouldn't be able to land. The jungle was too dense to cut. There was no way in the middle of the triple-canopy jungle that they'd be spotted from the air. Smoke grenades would be useless. The only way out was for the men to descend the cliff and hump out four or five klicks just to fashion a landing zone before any chopper could get to them.

Avery sat in the middle of the group of men, who huddled close. He whispered, "We'll take up position in twos, twenty meters apart, parallel to the top of the ridge. Sullivan and Catchahorse, take the north end. Zabriski and Hill, you take the south. Me and Spellbinder'll be in the middle. Don't anybody do nothin'. Don't move, don't smoke. Just kill leeches. When it's quiet, I'm gonna recon the Trail. When Charlie has moved on, Hill and Zabriski can take their pictures. Not until I give the all-clear. I'll let you know what I find. . ." The last thing he said was, "The password's 'Can't get no . . .'"

"'Satisfaction.'" They all heard Marcus whisper the reply.

They crawled off beneath the low vegetation to their positions. Peter and Marcus found a small space where they took off the heavy web belts, which held their machetes and canteens. Slowly and very quietly they pulled magazines from their bandoleers, laying them out, side by side, in neat rows within arm's reach. They checked that there was film in their cameras, then they sat down again as they'd done a hundred times before, back to back. It's what kept them sane in an insane situation—whispering to each other over their shoulders. Marcus lit up a joint and took three or four quick hits before he passed it to Peter.

Smoking the grass made what they witnessed next seem more freaky than normal. In the few minutes the two of them had been there, tiny inch-long tree leeches had covered their bodies from head to toe. Neither had ever seen so many leeches on one place before. It seemed like they had been living on the leaves of the bushes, thirsting for human blood, waiting for the men to show up. They hopped, ten at a time, onto the men's arms and legs and faces. Once they were on the skin, each one quickly puffed up with blood to the size of a marble. After they burst, they left behind a pool of blood to drip and dry. In no time, they were covered with blood, with their shirts and pants turned the same reddish brown as their skin. There were so many leeches it was pointless to try to do anything about them. It seemed as if the men were going to be bled dry. Peter imagined that a special United Nations task force would be sent to find their bodies thirty years after the war had ended. All they would find were tiny piles of the silver fillings from their teeth—and the leeches crawling among them, pissed off because there was nothing more to suck on. It was the marijuana that made him envision a miniature model of Stonehenge composed of tooth fillings constructed by leeches.

34

The act of waiting is something soldiers have always learned to be good at. In Vietnam smoking a joint was the usual way to kill time. The marijuana helped Peter slide into a dream.

It was his first spring at Yale—May 1967—only a year earlier. The rain from a warm spring thunderstorm was whipped in sheets against the ancient lead-paned window. Whenever the lightning flashed, the sky outside turned from dark gunmetal gray to iridescent white.

Peter stood at a podium in a writing class held in a damp limestone room on the second floor of a building overlooking the green. The room was barely lit by two small ceiling fixtures with dusty lightbulbs. Peter found it difficult to see the words on the paper in front of him. He turned the switch on the small brass light fixture at the top of the podium.

There was a vibrant and palpable energy in the room partially caused by the thunderstorm outside and partially due to the emotional charge from the students. He read slowly, laboriously, wanting not just to mouth the words but to clearly express the meaning beneath them. The essay was about a war raging on the opposite side of the world in a country called Vietnam. "We sit like privileged peas in our comfortable pod while a Buddhist monk pours gasoline over himself and lights himself on fire . . ."

Suddenly a bolt of lightning hit a tree outside. The room reverberated with the thunder echoing off the limestone buildings in the quadrangle. Peter paused to look out the window. Everyone's eyes followed his. Then he went on to finish the essay. "The monk is transformed from a living, breathing man into a pile of lifeless ash."

A boy sitting in the back row let out a ruthless howl, but Peter kept reading, "The monk, still alive, remains motionless, even as his molecules explode . . ."

The boy in the back jeered even louder.

Peter raised his voice to make sure he would be heard, ". . . transforming himself, from man into God, performing the ultimate sacrifice . . . sacrificing his life so others might live . . ."

This time the boy in back stood up and shouted angrily, "Are you saying we should set ourselves on fire?" The others in the class rallied behind the protester. Peter looked up from the podium, searching the back of the room for the boy.

Another boy spoke out, "I don't like this war any more than you do. I'm going on to law school to defend *your* right not to go."

". . . where you'll be safe from the draft for another five years!" Peter yelled back.

"If you believe so strongly about what we're doing in Vietnam, Mr. Hill, why don't you join up?"

The boy's remarks struck Peter right in the gut.

Someone in the front row threw a pack of matches up at the podium, "Why don't you light yourself on fire, Hill?"

"Yeah, Hill . . . come on, baby, light my fire!"

Peter stood frozen at the podium, knowing he had written on a politically charged issue, but having no idea his essay was going to produce such passion. The class was in a fervor but he continued anyway, not knowing if he could be heard above the voices. This time, as he began to speak, a loud clap of thunder quieted the classroom. "The point is, I watched this monk on television, from the comfort of my bed. I watched as he poured a can of gasoline over himself and lit a match—that same simple act we all perform each time we light a cigarette."

"Come on, baby, light my *fire!*" the boy in front started to sing.

"Don't you people get it?" Peter's voice was at a high pitch.

Some of the boys and girls in the back started to pound out the rhythm to the song by the Doors, "Couldn't get much *high-er!*"

Pandemonium broke out. The class stormed the podium. Marcus ran up to help defend his best friend. He grabbed the boy who'd charged up from the back row by the shirt and threw him down hard. Everyone stopped when they heard the boy's head crack against the hardwood floor. They looked down in disbelief at the river of blood flowing from his head. Suddenly it felt like the war had come closer—as if it was being fought right there in New Haven, Connecticut.

The next morning Peter and Marcus walked a few blocks off the Yale campus into downtown New Haven and enlisted in the army.

35

The two recruits were ordered to report to the railroad station in New Haven in two weeks' time, at seven o'clock on a Saturday morning. The tall and polished recruiting sergeant told them that there they would receive their transfer orders from a Captain Connelly.

Neither was prepared for what they met up with at the station. It turned out to be an ice-cold morning in November 1967, with the war and the antiwar protest movement raging with equal ferocity. The Reverend Daniel Berrigan, a chaplain at Yale, had organized the largest peace march ever held on the same Saturday that Peter and Marcus were ordered to report for induction.

As they approached the station, their taxi was quickly swallowed up by a sea of protesters flooding the parking lot. They had created a human barricade across the front of the building. Police were everywhere. Police in riot gear, police on horseback, police positioned on top of patrol cars and vans, and police in the process of handcuffing protesters and stuffing them into vans. Marcus and Peter and the others weren't even in the army, but it seemed to them as if they had already arrived at the battlefield. The long-haired students held their faces up to the taxi windows yelling, "Baby killers, baby killers!" Their cab was forced to follow close behind two mounted police. It was one of the worst thousand-yard trips either of them had ever taken. Seeing their classmates among the crowd made Peter and Marcus doubt their decision to go. Inside the station they joined about thirty other enlistees who surrounded Captain Connelly in a tight circle. The captain was a young man in his early twenties and clearly overwhelmed but he did his best to keep the men calm. One red-faced recruit with a shaved head yelled back at the line of protesters who had squeezed into the station and were being pinned against a wall by the police. The recruit gave them the finger, holding both his hands high over his head. "Fucking three-toed chickens!" he yelled at them, referring to the peace signs they waved in the air. Captain Connelly, shouting above the battle raging all around him, valiantly told his men in a much-resigned tone, "Believe it or not, gentlemen, those of you who go to Vietnam will be fighting for the freedom of these very people to protest the war."

For the first time, Peter knew he had joined a society that had to answer to a higher power. He suddenly found himself part of a world with a much more far-reaching set of rules than he had ever been subjected to. As he was embarking to supposedly fight for the freedom of his country, he was shocked to find that, oddly enough, he had given up almost all of his own personal freedom. In a nutshell, he was a private in the U.S. Army, and there were about three million men and women above him in the chain of command who could tell him what to do! It was a sobering thought—something he considered on the train all the way from New Haven to Fort Dix, New Jersey, where they were headed for basic training.

36

Peter watched a leech puff up to the size of a grape, let go, and roll off his forearm.

Marcus whispered over his shoulder to him. "I'm feeling so fuckin' freaky lately—since I got back from Bangkok. Just don't know what it is."

"Couldn't be the dope, could it?" Peter whispered back.

"Who the fuck knows. It's like I'm feeling I'm not of this world anymore. It's weird, like I'm not attached or something . . ." His thought trailed off.

"I'm slightly freaked out myself," admitted Peter.

"You got an excuse—yer in love."

Peter leaned forward, turned around, and looked at Marcus.

Marcus smiled. "I know you, man. We've been together a lot of years. We went to school together. There ain't nothin' I don't know about you. And I know what yer looking for is trouble."

"She's the first white woman I've seen in six months . . ."

"You want her bad."

"I don't know . . ."

"You want her."

"So you want the truth?" Peter asked.

Marcus smiled, "That's our deal, man."

"I feel something—okay? And it's heavy, very heavy. But it's like, I can't afford to *feel* this much—not here, not now."

"Read you loud and clear."

"I don't know what to fucking do about it."

"What-*ever*, man. Whatever you feel like . . ."

Peter turned around to look at Marcus's face—a face that seemed both old and young at the same time. Marcus with his mustache that was so blond you could hardly tell he had a mustache at all. Marcus who always looked happy but had always carried with him an inexorable sadness that went deep down, way beneath his light blond hair and tanned California surfer skin. But it was Marcus's sadness that made Peter feel close to him. It had always been this way with Marcus—his sadness reeled people in.

Peter said, "When I'm with her—or when I'm not with her—it's like she's inside me or some fucking thing. It's like she crawled through my skin like a fucking leech. That's not what I mean—you know what I mean, goddamnit!"

But Peter felt Marcus didn't know. Marcus looked back anyway, happy for his friend.

Peter went on, his emotion so strong it rattled around the bushes. "She's right here, man. Right now. Right fucking *now*. How can I afford to *feel* this shit?" Peter questioned, ". . . right here, right by this fucking trail . . ."

There was a long silence before Marcus spoke, "Wish I was in love, man. Right now I don't feel *nothin'* for *nothin'*. It's like I'm invisible, man."

"You remember what Joe Rice told us in English class?" Peter asked him. "Remember that book by James Jones, about Pearl Harbor?"

Marcus stared blankly. "Naw, don't remember shit, man."

"Don't matter . . ."

"So what'd he say?"

"Just some shit . . . It's all shit, ain't it?"

"Truly," said Marcus.

Peter held out the front of his shirt so he could peer down inside at his chest. Dozens of tiny tree leeches had made their home on his skin. Several were already puffed up like miniature balloons filled with blood.

"Leechville."

Marcus pulled a small plastic bottle of insect repellent from his helmet band and handed it to his friend. Peter squirted some down under his shirt. Then he tried to hand the bottle back to Marcus.

Marcus pushed his hand away. "Keep it," he said.

"Yer not gonna use it?"

"Don't need it.

"Marcus—yer getting strange in yer old age."

"Stranger, man. I was born strange."

"Stranger in a strange land."

"You know when we were in school . . . we always talked about what we were gonna do with our lives."

"Yeah."

"Well, man, I never thought I was gonna amount to anything."

"But you used to say . . ."

"It's not what I felt inside."

"Don't matter what you do, it only matters who you are."

"Joe used to say that."

"Now I'm saying it for him," Peter said. ". . . Shhh!"

They heard voices through the bushes and immediately, they were back on edge. Marcus got up on his knees. He turned around and whispered to Peter, "Gotta find out what we're here for." Holding his camera at the ready, he disappeared into the leaves. He was gone before Peter could say anything. If he'd had the chance, Peter would've told him not to go. He felt it wasn't time yet.

The moment after Marcus had gone Peter felt that danger like a cold clammy hand had touched his back. Very quietly Peter took his weapon off safe and positioned it to cover Marcus on the trail. Then he sat stone-still, waiting for him to return.

As Peter listened for some sound of Marcus returning from the trail, a centipede, about a foot long, had crawled up the outside of his shirt and quickly wrapped itself around his neck. He reached up to grab it even before his brain had fully registered what it was. He flung it down with a shiver. When he saw it on the ground, he chopped at it with his machete, insanely cutting it into as many pieces as he could and watched, disgusted, as its parts ran off in different directions. "It's a bad sign," Peter whispered to himself. "I'm going to check on Marcus . . ." Then all hell broke loose. A barrage of gunfire came from deep in the jungle across the trail. Peter heard his friend's M-16 fire a quick burst in return. Then it went silent.

AK-47 bullets ripped through the leaves just above Peter's head. He clung to the ground hearing return fire coming from Avery's position to his left. Before he could return fire, Peter heard rustling in the bushes beside him. Immediately he rolled onto his back, aiming his weapon at the noise, his finger ready to squeeze the trigger. But then he heard the words, "Can't get no . . ."

"Satisfaction," he said, relieved to see Catchahorse, who had low-crawled through the bushes.

"Charlie's here."

"No shit, Kemosabee!"

More bullets ripped through the leaves just above their heads. Catchahorse lifted his weapon about to return fire . . . "Wait!" Peter pulled his barrel down. "Zabriski's out there. He went to get a picture."

"I'll take a look," said Catchahorse.

"No," said Peter, heading into the bushes, "I'll go."

Catchahorse followed right behind him. After only two or three meters, the leaves ended and suddenly they were looking out across a narrow dirt road—a road that could've been somewhere in the hills of Connecticut, except for one thing—Marcus's body lay riddled with bullet holes, facedown in the dirt.

On impulse, Peter started toward him, without thinking what he was doing. Catchahorse grabbed his shirt and held him back. "He's not moving, man—looks like he was hit in the head."

"I've got to see."

"He looks dead."

Peter lunged forward, diving out onto the trail. "Marcus," he called. Nothing. No answer. Peter saw the open wound in the back of his head.

"Get back, Hill," said Catchahorse.

A single shot buried itself into Marcus's side. It made his body shimmy like a car going over a bump.

Peter ran on all fours back into the bush while Catchahorse fired a volley back across the trail.

Peter looked into Catchahorse's deep brown eyes. "He was hit in the head. We've got to get his camera—at least his camera. He got *killed* for that fucking picture." Before Catchahorse could respond, Peter crawled back out, hooking Marcus's camera strap with the end of his barrel. A volley of shots rang out—this time aimed at Avery's position. Peter dived into the bushes beside Catchahorse again.

Catchahorse slammed in another magazine, "Shit, I thought you bought it, man! You gotta forget about Zabriski. We ain't never gonna get him . . ."

"He's my friend . . ." Again Peter looked into Catchahorse's kind eyes. "For what, man?" Peter said, "for a fuckin' picture?" He put Marcus's camera strap over his head.

A long volley of shots rang out from the trail. Suddenly there was a sound behind them. Catchahorse and Peter both spun around and instantly had Avery in their sites. "Jeesus!" said Avery. "Do I look *Vietnamese*, fuckhead?" he said to both of them.

"Zabriski bought it," Catchahorse informed him. "He's on the trail."

"Motherfucker! What the fuck was he *doin'* out there? Now get yer asses down the cliff before we all get wasted. I'll wait till you guys are down."

"But Marcus. He's lying out there," Peter said.

Avery looked at the camera hanging from Peter's neck. "That's his? He got the pictures? We can go."

Catchahorse whispered something in Avery's ear.

"We can't risk losing another man," Avery said, looking into Peter's eyes.

"I can't leave him."

Avery grabbed Peter's shirt. "You *will*."

Without saying a word, Catchahorse bolted quickly out through the bushes toward the trail. Immediately, another volley of enemy fire rang out.

"Fuck!" said Avery. "Fuck, fuck!"

Avery raced after Catchahorse. He returned quickly as more shots ripped through the bushes. Sullivan appeared. Avery looked at Sullivan and Peter through steely eyes. "You guys get the fuck down the cliff!"

"What happened to Kemosabee?" asked Sullivan.

"Waddaya fuckin' think?" answered Avery. "Move it!"

Peter knew this would be his last chance. Before Avery could stop him, he lunged through the bushes toward the trail. He fought his way through the underbrush, blindly firing in the direction of the trail as he went. The barrel on his M-16 grew so hot it sizzled against the leaves it touched. He was out of control with anger. He couldn't see the men he was firing at, but he sensed their position as they fired back at him. At one point he knew he'd silenced at least one fucking Vietnamese forever. It felt good. He jammed in another magazine, pushing himself on his stomach under the bushes. When he saw light in front of him he knew he was almost there. He inched farther into the leaves until he saw the sunlight coming from above the trail. Finally, peering through the leaves, he saw Marcus's body lying just a few meters in front of him.

Suddenly he heard Avery and Sullivan firing madly from behind him. This was his chance. He pulled himself forward, his face scraping through the wet dirt like a plow. The covering fire worked. He dragged the body back into the bushes by the legs. He was glad it had been by the legs because he didn't want to have to look at his friend's face.

Avery and Sullivan kept firing while Peter struggled to pull Marcus back through the thick brush. When he reached the top of the cliff, Catchahorse lay at Avery's feet. Avery had found his body in the bushes. He had made it partway back before he'd caught a bullet in the back. Spellbinder lay beside him.

Peter looked into Avery's angry eyes then turned away. He rolled Marcus's body up to the cliff. He knew that if he hesitated he wouldn't be able to do what he needed to. Before he had time to think about it, he gave him a hard shove with his boot until his body disappeared over the edge. There was no sound after that, of Marcus falling or hitting the bottom. It was like he'd disappeared into a void. Avery and Sullivan pushed Catchahorse and Spellbinder over. Spellbinder's fall was terrible. It sounded like he landed directly on his head—they heard the loud crack of his skull hitting the rocks below.

"Let's get the fuck outta here," Avery whispered. "You guys go first."

Peter followed Sullivan, inching down the steep cliff.

The three survivors began the slow descent. They saw Marcus first. His body hadn't made it all the way down. His shirt had hooked itself on a tree branch, which left him dangling out of reach above the ravine. His head was cocked to the side at a weird angle as if he was looking at something. Peter noticed his Spider-Man comic sticking out of his pant pocket.

When the three reached the pool, they stopped to fill their canteens beneath the spider's web. After what had just happened the spider seemed of little consequence. What they really wanted to do was to move as quickly as they could, away from that place. They had nothing to say to each other. There were no words that could dig deep enough to explain what had happened. Even Avery seemed different after being up on the trail. As Peter thought of what had just taken place, he began to seethe with hate for Jake Broward. The unanswerable question *What had Marcus died for?* sat in the pit of Peter's stomach. Could it have been for a good reason—for any reason at all? He couldn't answer yes. Starting on the climb down from the trail, and continuing for days and months and years afterward, Peter found rationales. If he hadn't, he felt for sure he would've have gone insane. Over and over, Peter would ask himself, *Why did we go there—what was the point?* Of all the ridiculous missions concocted in Vietnam, he thought their walk in the woods might've been the most hideous. To make himself feel better, he desperately wanted to think of another incident that was even more ridiculous, even more bizarre—even more pointless. He once saw a major swing out of a light observation helicopter and get the top of his head chopped off—the spinning blades flinging the major's steel pot off, with part of his head in it. But that incident was caused by the man's own stupidity. Their mission happened through no choice of their own.

37

The journey down the cliff seemed to go much faster. Maybe it was because of all that had happened that they hardly noticed the difficult climb down. When they reached the bottom, the light was gone. None of them had said a word all the way down. Finally, Sullivan, exhausted, said, "We gotta stop, I can't move another foot."

Avery didn't argue. "About time somebody said something. I would've just kept going."

They were in a kind of limbo—not knowing where in the world they were. They were in total blackness. They had come down as far as the sloping forest where the floor was soft and damp. It was cold. They could feel the cold trunks of the trees as they passed. There was little to keep warm with but they were exhausted enough to need to lie down immediately and sleep. They lay side to side with their shoulders touching just to feel secure knowing there was another human being on earth. Peter sensed that even Avery felt the fright of the place. There were noises out there, whatever small sounds an animal made; they listened to them bounce around between the tops of the tall trees and the trunks. Even the insect sounds were loud. Then nothing. Then just the white light that sometimes comes behind the eyes when sleep comes quickly.

In the morning they retraced their path through the trees. In the back of their minds they knew they were taking a big chance—they should have cut a new trail. Every soldier knows you never take the same trail back. But they were too tired to bother.

They forded the stream at the place where Avery had killed the leech. Sullivan walked point. Avery walked last. As Sullivan pulled himself up the far embankment, he grabbed the same small tree they had all used before to lower themselves down into the water. The tree was perfectly placed for a handhold. This was the kind of thing Charlie expected. Charlie knew they would be back. He even knew they would be tired enough to cross the stream in the exact same spot. He knew someone would grab on to that tree. Peter was just approaching the stream, still in the elephant grass, when it happened. He never saw the blast, which was hidden by the tall grass. It didn't shake the ground. The sound was muffled—like a dull thud. He and Avery both knew that Sullivan had set off a booby trap. They knew, without even looking, exactly where Charlie had set the trap. When the two of them came out of the grass they found Sullivan floating facedown in the stream.

The bright red color of Sullivan's blood contrasted with the bright green vegetation on the far bank. Avery came up and stood next to Peter and the two of them just stared down at him for a while. Finally Avery stepped down into the water and pushed Sullivan's body across the surface to the other side. It looked like he was sliding him across a piece of glass. Peter walked across and helped Avery drag the body up the embankment and into the tall grass. They sat down on the bank and smoked a Camel. Avery made a note of the location on the map so a chopper could return for the body. Then they continued to head back toward the laager. There were still at least twenty kilometers to go. The two men could not have carried Sullivan that far. So Sullivan became another body they left in the field.

It was nightfall when Peter and Avery finally reached the laager where the mission had begun. A Huey sat on one side of the clearing ready to fly a dozen grunts, together with their heavy packs, back to Chu Lai. The Huey's rotors were already picking up speed as Avery and Peter managed to squeeze onboard. Its engine revved. Its blades bit as hard as they could at the thick evening air, but there was simply too much weight to lift off the ground. The crew chief told Peter and Avery they'd have to get off and catch a chopper in the morning.

Avery lifted his carbine, slowly and seriously, pressing the side of the barrel against the chief's cheek. The chief told the pilot to try again. The bird inched forward on its skids across the grass. There was a tree line bordering the clearing on all sides. As it began to pick up speed, they headed directly for the trees at the end of the clearing. Neither Peter nor Avery doubted that the chopper would make it into the sky. Nobody on that chopper was willing to spend another night out there in Weirdsville. At the last second, the pilot pulled the stick hard to the left. The Huey spun and headed back across the clearing, now a just a meter off the ground. By the time the chopper reached the tree line on the far side, it had picked up enough speed to make it three-quarters of the way up the trees, nearer the tops where the branches were thinner. The blades cut a path through the trees, like some mad barber's shears, sending them sailing out into the sunset beyond. It was a small miracle that they made it but the truth was that everyone aboard was too tired, and too jaded, to make a big deal of it. It was as if they all just expected miracles while their tired minds engaged in other thoughts of other places. Peter thought about leaving Marcus's body up at the trail. As he listened once again to the familiar chop of the rotor blades beating against the air, he felt a deep sadness in the pit of his stomach, a feeling that would never leave him.

38

When Peter returned to life on LZ Danger, he felt as if nothing was the same. The monotony of army life that had once held a feeling of safety for him was no longer to be counted on. After the trail, the bizarre became normal. He had changed. The loss of Marcus was so huge that everything else seemed petty. One night Peter was nearly killed by a drunken soldier. The guy had sprayed a full magazine into the wall of the PIO hootch, the line of bullets leaving a line of holes in the half-inch plywood under Peter's cot. Three bullets had gone right through the jerry can he kept next to his cot. When he saw it in the morning, the water was drained out down to the three holes. Peter ran after him and found him lying on the ground, puking. He had been drinking because he'd just reenlisted for another twelve months in Vietnam.

The army, with its anal need to be orderly, had sent out a cleanup mission—twenty or so men—to recover the bodies left at the trail. The brigade chaplain held an informal funeral service. He read from a mimeographed piece of paper on which was written in official army language something about the men having been part of a reconnaissance mission to a suspected NVA base camp west of Chu Lai. That was the official location of the mission—*west of Chu Lai*.

Marcus, Catchahorse, Spellbinder, and Sullivan had all been killed on a mission that didn't exist. Did that mean they hadn't really been killed at all—that they weren't really dead? Peter wondered what the army wrote on their records, because Marcus, Kemosabee, and Spellbinder had all died in Laos.

But they were dead—so it didn't matter. Nothing seemed to matter anymore. All Peter wanted was to forget. To stay stoned and forget. He went where everyone on the LZ went for that—to P. J. Santa's photo lab.

P. J. had been a grunt in the infantry who had secured a job on the LZ after he had written a letter about his narcolepsy to his congressman back in Rhode Island. He told the congressman he didn't feel safe being in the field where he might fall asleep, anywhere at any time. He fell asleep once during a firefight, which he said actually saved his life. After it had ended, Charlie had counted him among the dead.

P. J. was a graduate of Rochester Institute of Technology and had been a student of the famous photographer Minor White. He carried a Leica—without an automatic exposure meter—with which he took far and away the best photographs of any of the division combat photographers. It was P.J.'s connection with his congressman that secured the photo lab that became the correspondents' and photographers' sanctuary—a sanctuary where they all went to forget about the war and get stoned. It also became the school where Santa taught the others to make beautiful black-and-white prints with the finest Kodak developing chemicals and printing papers that the army's money could buy.

But mostly the photo lab was a place of refuge from the bullshit army itself. Sitting in air-conditioned comfort on relaxing canvas chairs, the men contemplated the earth at the speed it slowly turned. They waited, for the simple, the inevitable—like the sun sinking beneath the horizon while they smoked the cigar-sized joints of marijuana dusted with opium. It seemed the perfect place from which to view the world outside. And also, there was the thought: *man walks on moon*, which could carry anyone away. Maybe it was just the dope but sometimes it seemed as if they were players in an old French film—set in Indochina in the 1950s. It was as if they had created a totally new reality—as if they were looking out through a bamboo curtain.

39

Eventually—maybe it was because he thought it would get him back on track—Peter decided to head out to LZ Strange again. The PIO had been radioed a report that the LZ had come under attack during the night. Peter should have known that *under attack* was an army euphemism. What had really happened was that LZ Danger had been overrun. Broward, of course, was long gone when it happened.

The place Peter saw when the chopper settled onto the pad did not look like the same place he and Kate had visited a few weeks earlier. The mountaintop was nearly devoid of human life. When the chopper landed, a cleanup detail consisting of a few men was gathering up M-16s, helmets, and bandoleers of ammunition, lining them up along the edge of the pad. There were small paper tags—the kind used to address parcels—tied with white string to each item in the row. As the chopper came in to land, Peter watched the small tags dance like whirling dervishes. They seemed to have a life of their own.

He asked a private what was going on.

"This is the last of them," he replied. "There were three choppers before. Pretty much everybody was wiped out. Pretty much everybody," he repeated his words as if he didn't quite believe them the first time.

Peter scratched a note in his book, "LZ—obliterated." He thought he might have made up a name for the place. The words rang like a cracked bell in his brain—but words alone could not explain what happened there.

What Peter saw next seemed like a scene written by Dante. A soldier was digging a hole to bury a pile of Vietnamese heads—probably twenty or thirty. Peter learned later that the GIs had put them on stakes around the perimeter like scarecrows to ward off the enemy. They took them down when the wind direction changed, bringing the smell back across the LZ.

Peter sat on the canvas bench seat of the Huey, his back against the quilted fabric insulating the engine wall, transfixed by the unreality that faced him. He didn't want to get out and set foot on the haunted ground; instead he sat in a state of shock listening to the Huey's blades relentlessly slicing the air above his head. He watched from his seat as the two soldiers piled the weapons, the helmets, and the bandoleers of ammo of the dead and wounded onto the metal floor.

Reluctantly, in order to make room, he stepped off. He saw what had once been a base camp for an American infantry company was now not much more than a barren piece of scorched earth on a hilltop. Sandbags and bent corrugated tin lay scattered everywhere. Slivers of metal from exploded mortars covered the ground. The men who remained were mostly invisible, hiding silently in their bunkers. The few who were out seemed to wander without focus, shuffling aimlessly among the debris. Nobody seemed to be in charge, or maybe nobody cared to be. The company had lost its spirit—its will as a fighting unit was gone. The men were no longer part of the 199th Light Infantry Brigade; they had become individuals again, lost within their own hearts and minds.

Peter could find nothing more to write in his small correspondent's notebook—nothing the army would print anyway—so he tucked it away in his pocket. He was taken in by the feeling of the place, but an army combat correspondent does not write about feelings—he takes down the names and hometowns of the heroes of the battle. He takes their pictures. He reports the enemy body count and the facts of how the firefight progressed—an accurate account of the action. But there, on LZ Strange where it had been an easy rout for Charlie, there was no story. The only body count had been American, another thing an army correspondent doesn't report.

In the light of day, the North Vietnamese were still firmly entrenched on a hilltop just a few hundred meters away, close enough so that the insignias on their green uniforms were visible to the naked eye. Charlie sat, mockingly, in full view of the Americans. Although the NVA had retreated to their mountaintop, they continued harassing with sporadic AK-47 fire. As the Huey pulled itself sadly into the sky carrying the last of the personal effects, an NVA sniper halfheartedly let go a few bursts. But as the chopper gained altitude, he stopped firing. The sniper wasn't trying to bring the chopper down. He didn't care about that chopper. By letting it go, it became a small victory because he knew what it was carrying belonged to soldiers already dead and wounded.

Peter walked along the perimeter, just inside the flimsy concertina wire the NVA had easily violated. He carried only his .45-caliber pistol and his Pentax camera. As he walked, a sad cloud of hopelessness settling over him, an NVA sniper started firing single shots that dug into the dirt at his feet. Strangely, Peter didn't run for cover. He didn't dive for the ground. He just kept walking. He felt bulletproof.

Finally Peter turned and looked straight out at the soldier who was shooting. A bullet spun off the ground six inches from his foot. He heard it ricochet off a piece of corrugated tin somewhere behind him. Another NVA soldier planted a flag on a bamboo pole beside the soldier who was shooting—the ultimate act of defiance. Peter lifted his Pentax to his eye and shot a picture. Then as he lowered his camera, he looked directly at the soldier to see what he would do. It was more an honest question than a dare.

Peter tried to make sense of all that had happened—as if he could, as if it was possible. As he continued to walk along the wire he saw the NVA set his gun down and look over at him. Peter thought he knew why the sniper stopped shooting, although he wasn't exactly sure—he wasn't exactly sure about anything anymore.

40

Peter's feet, in his Nike running shoes, rested on the coffee table in Gisella's office. His hands were folded behind his head. Gisella looked concerned. "Did you want him to shoot you, Peter?"

He listened to her words but wasn't ready to answer.

"Did you *want* to die?"

"I should've waved at the guy. I really should've waved. Wish I had it to do all over again . . ."

"You feel you'd like to have another chance . . . to do it right?"

He pondered her question. "Why yes, why of course," he said, sarcastically. "I'd remake the whole war—I'd make it happen in Hollywood. I'd be the star and"—he pulled his hands down from behind his head, took his feet off the table and sat up ramrod military straight on the edge of the couch—"and nobody would get killed." He felt his eyes fill with tears and yet he didn't cry. Instead, he took a deep breath, and turning to Gisella he asked, "Do you want to know what happened?"

Gisella nodded.

"After I smiled at the guy—after I'd reached some kind of understanding with him—this fucking F-4 Phantom jet dived right down out of nowhere and dropped a thousand-pound bomb on him. The guy didn't even hear it coming—neither of us did. He was still looking at me. He flew right up out of his hole. Pieces of him—his arms went one way, his legs went another way. His head went straight up—like it was going into orbit or something. It must've gone up a hundred feet." Peter stared blankly into Gisella's eyes. "I swear, he still had a smile on his face. What was weirdest of all was that he was looking at me with that same fucking smile on his face."

Gisella didn't speak. The two of them simply sat for a while—each of them feeling alone in the world. "It's strange," he said, "but I was always seeing faces of death."

41

Peter and Avery stood at the developing tray—their faces lit eerily by the red light of the photo lab darkroom. Peter picked up an eleven- by fourteen-inch piece of photographic paper with a pair of tongs, dropping it into a tray of developing solution. Then the two of them eagerly waited for an image to appear. As the thick trees of the jungle darkened on the paper, Peter swished it around in the tray to speed up the developing. Then they saw it . . .

"Look at that!" Avery cheered. "They're fuckin' American Deuce-and-a-halfs! On the fuckin' Ho Chi Minh Trail for chrissakes! Our fuckin' trucks!"

They looked at each other in the red light. "Marcus got the picture," Peter cheered.

"This'll fuck Broward right up his ass!"

Peter lifted the photo from the tray and dropped it into the fixing bath.

"I've got to tell Kate."

Avery frowned. Peter saw Avery knew something he wasn't saying.

"Remember, she's working on this story," Peter reminded him.

Avery told him, "She left for Thailand. She called to let you know."

Peter was crushed. He felt like he'd been shot in the chest. "What? In the middle of it all? She split? And you didn't tell me?"

"She's dangerous, Peter. Watch yer ass with her—she eats fuckin' guys like you for lunch."

"Yeah, well, I've got to find out for myself. I guess I'll take my R&R in Bangkok."

"Are you crazy, man?" It wasn't a question Peter was going to answer. "She's not gonna be waiting for you, man. She's gonna be with some dude. Everybody goes to Bangkok for only one fuckin' reason . . ."

"To find the most beautiful girl in the world."

"Yer crazy man—*dinki dow*."

42

"My God, Marcus!" Peter woke himself up with these words before he remembered he was on the Pan Am flight to Bangkok. Dreaming that he was back at Yale, he had been staring down at a pool of blood on the floor—the blood that had leaked from the head of the boy Marcus had hit.

His eyes opened and the dream stopped. He felt paralyzed. The left side of his forehead felt like it was glued to the window. He turned his eyes out, becoming lost in the beauty of the immense cloud formations that rose up above the turquoise sea. A bolt of lightning lit up the sky, drawing a bright line from the anvil top of a cloud down to the black water. The flash turned the color of the clouds from dark gray to pure silk white. For some reason—he couldn't remember why—he was reminded of Yale again.

Peter's eyelids turned heavy again while the scene at the trail played itself out one more time. He fought to keep his eyes open so he wouldn't have to be there in the jungle. Suddenly, the world became far more beautiful than he'd ever seen it before. The clouds glowed with colors so subtle he was convinced that nobody else could see them. He saw colors he knew for certain didn't exist within the normal spectrum—soft pink that melted into shades of blue and green so luminescent it hurt his eyes to look at them.

43

In Peter's eyes the most beautiful girl in the world stood with him under a steaming shower in his bathroom at the Siam Hotel in Bangkok. Her name was Pen and she had long mahogany-colored hair. Helping her with her shampoo, he reveled in the delicious hot water raining down their bodies. It had been six months since he'd been in a hot shower. When Pen lifted her arm to pull back her hair he saw for the first time a line of scars, which ran like rungs on a ladder from her wrist almost to her shoulder. "Who did this to you?" Peter asked, incredulous.

"GI cut me for each friend he lose in Vietnam," Pen said sadly.

He asked her if she'd called the police, feeling the anger of the war return to his throat in an instant.

"He say he kill me if I tell," she told him with tears in her eyes.

Peter gently lifted her arm to his lips, kissing each scar once, thinking he might help heal her wounds. He couldn't help but wonder, as he held her arm, about all the nameless victims of Vietnam. It was strange how the war had left its marks on this beautiful girl. How many more marks was it going to make, he wondered—on how many people?

"I think we should go out—to a club," Peter said. "I am looking for someone—a woman," he told her.

"But you have me." She looked up, confused.

"This is different." he said. "It's business. She's Australian. A reporter."

"California Bar." She smiled. "Australians go there."

A light evening rain made the neon-lit streets of Bangkok glisten. There was a raw sexuality in the damp air as Mr. Kim, the driver Peter had hired, drifted his Toyota through the dreamy blurred lights of Bangkok's nightclub district. Bar girls stood dressed for work smoking cigarettes in doorways while the harsh notes of too-loud rock-and-roll music poured out of the clubs. The primitive beat of drums seemed to announce the sexual rituals that attracted GIs by the thousands.

Mr. Kim pulled up in front of the California Bar. Instead of getting out, he reached across the front seat to open the back door for his two passengers. Peter was reminded again how strikingly beautiful Pen was as she stepped onto the sidewalk in her simple black dress and high heels. She wore no jewelry at all. He thought that a chain of gold would set off her dark skin. He made a mental note to buy her one. Peter, dressed in clothes he picked up at the in Cam Rhan Bay PX, felt like he had just landed from another planet. He wore a lime-green Jack Nicklaus golf shirt that was at least a size too big for him, and a pair of white polyester pants. The only part of his outfit he didn't detest were his shoes—a pair of brown woven-leather Mexican huaraches that proved to be very comfortable. Pen pressed her soft palm into his as they tiptoed across a puddle on the sidewalk. A finger of cigarette smoke floated out through the open door, wrapping itself around them, dragging them inside. The California Bar was packed from wall to wall with GIs, all of whom were sporting a look similar to Peter's. Groups of Thai girls danced mostly among themselves to a rendition of the Rolling Stones' song "Satisfaction." The members of a slick-looking Filipino band were dressed in white sequined costumes that sparkled under the lights on a small stage in the center of the room. The lead singer, a thin boy who could've passed for a girl, expertly mimicked Mick Jagger's moves.

Almost immediately, Peter saw Kate dancing in a far corner of the room, her head leaning up against Randy Guest's chest. Randy's chubby hand grasped a glass of whiskey against her back. In his other hand he held a lit cigarette. Seeing her with him made Peter want to puke. He followed the Thai hostess to a table and angrily sat down in a chair she pulled out for him. Peter held her by the arm before she could get away and yelled over the loud music, "A sloe gin fizz and two vodka tonics for me."

While they waited for their drinks, Peter tried not to watch Kate dancing. "Satisfaction" ended with the band seamlessly segueing into "You Can't Always Get What You Want," with the tiny lead singer imitating Mick Jagger sucking on the microphone. Peter watched Kate and Randy return to their table as he emptied the first of his two vodkas. Feeling it was impossible for him to stay away from Kate for even a second longer, he suddenly bolted out of his chair, leaving Pen, and rushed across the dance floor toward her table.

Kate's face lit up with surprise when she saw him. "Peter . . . what are you doing here? I didn't expect . . ."

"You love this old fuck, don't you?" Peter cut her off, so angry he could spit. "Why didn't you tell me before I . . ." Suddenly, Peter felt the effects of the alcohol together with the anger pumping blood into his brain, making it difficult for him to speak. He mumbled something incoherently before he was able to get to his point, "You fuck with my heart for a few days, then go back to Daddy? Is that it? You're a bitch, Kate, a fucking bitch!"

Randy stood up, teetering, steadying himself with a hand on the table. "Wait a minute," he said, red-faced. "Who do you think you're talking to?"

Both confused and hurt, Peter aimed a punch at Randy's face. Shocked at the blood that immediately flowed from his nose, Peter stepped back, too drunk to notice Randy expertly preparing to punch Peter hard in the stomach. The next thing Peter knew, he was doubled over on the floor with the wind knocked out of him. Through his blurred vision, he made out Kate's face inches in front of his. She was kneeling beside him. He saw her turn to look back at Randy, who loomed above him. Randy spoke, looking down at Peter: "I'm not ex-actly sure what this is all about. I could guess but I'm not sure I even want to know."

Kate told him, "This is Sergeant Hill you just punched out, Randy—the guy who saved us from the NVA."

"I know bloody well who it was I punched out, dear. The same bloke who unbuttoned your pants in Chu Lai—wasn't it?" He walked away speaking mostly to himself. "I'll dress my bloody wounds at the bloody bar over a bloody double."

Two American military policemen appeared, quickly picking Peter up off the floor, spiriting him to a back room, where they laid him out on a table. One of them pulled out his wallet to check his ID.

Peter, as if in a dream, heard one of the MPs speak. "Sergeant Peter Bartholomew Hill, U.S. Army Combat Correspondent."

"He's been under a lot of stress of late," Kate said.

"Haven't they all though."

"You're a sweet fellow."

"Is he with you?"

"Yes. I'll take him back to his hotel."

"Get him out of here or he'll land in a Thai jail. They won't be as kind."

While the band played "Sympathy for the Devil" Kate and Pen each took an arm and walked Peter across the dance floor to the en-trance. Randy swiveled around on his barstool as they passed by the bar. He and Kate had nothing to say to each other. He let out a long stream of cigarette smoke, watching the three walk out the door.

Outside, under the awning, Kate asked Pen where they were staying.

When Pen said the name of the hotel, "Siam," it evoked much more than just the name of a hotel. The way she pronounced the word, *Zi-yam*, reminded Kate what she loved about this part of the Orient. It was damp and dark—and, yes, evil. It was a place she knew she could hide in and not be ashamed at anything she might do or feel. She felt her own dark thoughts were easily hidden. There in the dark shadows, her shame suddenly disappeared. She allowed herself to look at Pen for the first time—to really look. She saw how extraordinarily beautiful she was.

"Get us a taxi, love," Kate said, watching her run into the rain to flag down a cab.

On the ride back Peter puked on the floor of the taxi. The driver was still swearing in Thai when they pulled up to the hotel.

Back in his room, the last thing Peter remembered before blanking out was someone wiping his face with a wet towel. Then he was gone.

Kate and Pen undressed and climbed into the huge bed beside Peter.

44

Peter awakened to the sound of the traffic coming through an open window. Kate leaned against the window wrapped in a white towel, looking down at the city. Peter attempted to sit up in bed but the throbbing in his temples forced him to lie back down.

"Feel pretty fucked up—huh? We brought you back last night in a taxi—you were covered with vomit."

"I don't remember. I must've blacked out. What happened?"

"You punched Randy. He punched you. End of story."

"That explains why my stomach feels like a twisted pretzel."

"That would make sense. That's where he punched you."

"Where did I punch him?"

"In the nose."

"Good."

Kate looked past Peter at Pen, who was just sitting up in the bed. "This is Pen," Kate said.

"I know."

"I thought you might have forgotten."

There was a knock on the door.

"What fun." Kate smiled. "Perhaps it's Randy."

"Maybe it's Broward," said Peter.

"Room service!" the voice came through the door.

169

Kate walked to the door and opened it. A young Thai waiter pushed a cart full of coffee and pastries into the room. Kate walked back and sat down again on the bed beside Pen. "I was going to explain about Randy before I left Chu Lai . . . I didn't want to spoil what you and I had."

"Our little fling?"

Kate grew angry, "Peter, I don't sleep with every man I meet!" Now she was truly hurt. "And to think I trusted you . . ."

"Well, what am I supposed to think? I fell for you, Kate. Goddamnit! I'm a dumb, dumb shit—ain't I?"

"Peter . . ."

"I am . . . aren't I?" He said, feeling sorry for himself.

"I felt an awful lot for you, Peter. In Chu Lai. And . . . I still do," Kate told him. "But I have a life in Saigon. I had it before I met you."

"More like a *history* than a life."

He could see she was hurt. "That's cruel, Peter."

"I'm sorry," he told her. "I don't know who to trust anymore."

"It's confusing as hell—isn't it," Kate said.

There was a knock on the door. Kate got up from the bed again to open it. Mr. Kim, the driver, stood in the hallway, smiling. "Time to meet Buddha!"

Kate turned to Peter and laughed, "Does this mean the end is near?"

Peter explained, "Mr. Kim is taking us to see the Golden Buddha."

"Oh, I'm glad that's all it is." Kate laughed.

"I hope you'll come," Peter told her.

He told Mr. Kim they'd meet him in the lobby in half an hour.

As Mr. Kim walked out, the waiter entered with more coffee. Kate returned to the bed and sat down beside Pen, who leaned back, naked, against the headboard. "God, she's got beautiful breasts," Kate said.

"So do you," Peter told Kate.

"Mine are less accessible."

"Like your heart."

"That's for protection."

"Like your affair with Broward."

"I told you," Kate frowned, "it was just . . ."

He cut her off. "Why did you fuck with him at all?"

"The dirty truth?"

"I'd like to know the truth about something."

"When I was new in-country, I used him—I knew he could be helpful to me."

"I guess I have a lot to learn," Peter said.

Kate touched his shoulder in a motherly way. "I'm glad you made it back alive, Peter."

"I thought you might be waiting when I got back," he said.

"I work for UPI. I couldn't just hang around."

"That's not the impression I get. You used me too. To get you to the A Shau Valley."

"Is that what you think, Peter? I would've gone to the Ho Chi Minh Trail with you if I could have."

"Broward wouldn't have allowed that. He wanted me dead . . . and you alive. Marcus didn't make it back."

Kate was stunned. "Marcus? He was killed? You never said . . ."

"Just me and Avery made it back. I'm sure we weren't supposed to—a minor glitch in Broward's plan. The others . . . we left their bodies at the trail."

"Peter, I'm really sorry . . ." She stroked the back of his head.

Kate kissed his temple. Peter stood up and looked for a cigarette, finding a pack of Camels on the dresser. He lit one for Kate and one for himself and sat back down on the bed.

"Remember the convoy on the way back from the temple? Marcus got pictures of the same trucks on the Ho Chi Minh Trail. They were the fuckers that killed him!"

Kate frowned and took a long drag on her cigarette.

"Don't you get it?" Peter was annoyed. "We were attacked by friendlies! Fucking ARVNs! Marcus was killed by the fucking South Vietnamese who are supposed to be on our fucking side!"

"Marcus got pictures of the trucks?"

"We have the photos—they were hauling fucking cinnamon, for chrissakes."

"Peter, you know what this means?"

"Yeah, I know what this means . . . my best friend was killed in a war nobody wants—for what—fucking cinnamon?"

Kate thought deeply. Finally she muttered, "Broward, Morgan, Tao . . ."

". . . Ho Chi fucking Minh!" Peter interrupted. "And, for what?"

Kate gave Peter a strange look.

"The stuff tastes like shit," Peter rambled on. "Cinna . . . fuckin'. . . min . . ." He laughed madly. "Ho . . . Chi . . . Cinna . . . Minh!" He flopped backward onto the bed.

"Peter, I'm starting to doubt *everything*—including my own sanity."

Peter looked at Kate. She seemed totally deflated. "We've got to catch Broward," Peter said.

"One thing I know—he's slimy enough to do almost anything."

"Almost?" Peter checked his watch. "It's time to pray—to Buddha."

"I don't know if I should go with you. You know how temples affect me." Kate smiled.

"Yeah, you actually start to *feel*."

"Peter, stop trying to hurt me—I feel bad enough already."

Pen got up off the bed and walked to the bathroom. Both Peter and Kate watched her turn on the shower and step in.

45

Bangkok Harbor bustled with activity. The strong rays of sunlight seemed hot enough to make the brown-tinted water boil. Peter with Kate, Pen, and Mr. Kim relaxed in a motorized sampan as it wove its way through the traffic of the crowded harbor toward the Golden Buddha Temple. As the noisy sampan plied through what looked more like syrup than water, Kate took pictures of everything. There were large freighters at anchor unloading their cargo into small sampans that clung like leeches to their hulls. The harbor seemed to have no rational order—still, it appeared that all the craziness of the small boats speeding back and forth between the ships and the docks and all the chaotic unloading and loading somehow made sense. It was as if the chaos were actually a kind of mystical order that could only be understood by the Eastern mind. After all, it was the Orient, and the Orient functioned with a set of natural laws different from the West.

How strange it was, Peter thought, that just a few hours from Vietnam, there existed a country where the people were actually at peace with each other. They smiled at one another. They seemed happy. Peter sat back against the padded red vinyl seat, put one arm around Kate, the other around Pen, and actually dared to feel happy for that moment in time—happier than he ever could have felt in Vietnam. Kate walked forward to take a picture of Peter and Pen. "Show me some love," she said pointing the long lens at them. "Let's see you kiss—you two!"

The visual effect of the white temple in the morning sun was dazzling. Thousands of pieces of colored glass embedded into the stucco glistened like Christmas tree lights. Mr. Kim waited on the dock with the sampan while Kate and Peter followed Pen inside. The contrast of the bright sun and the dark inside was extreme. It was the difference between loud and quiet. White and black. Maybe it was the difference between the West and the East, Peter thought. It was nearly impossible to see in the dark. But as their eyes began to adjust, they found themselves in the presence of hundreds of monks prostrated at the feet of a giant gold statue of Buddha, their saffron-orange robes glowing in the light of hundreds of candles. Pen, wrapped in just a piece of yellow silk, looking more beautiful than ever, walked confidently up to the altar while the sea of monks chanted their doleful mantra. She took three joss sticks, handing one to Peter and one to Kate, which they placed in the sand in the pots beneath the statue. The three kneeled on the cool terrazzo floor to pray, with Buddha sitting above them, resplendent, pure, simple, smiling, all-knowing, glimmering, gold. Gazing down upon them, His presence, even as a statue, held them captive beneath His downturned eyes. Pen kneeled between them holding on to their hands as if she were the connection between them. It seemed to Peter that their hands were all that tied Pen to this world. Without Kate and him to hold her, he imagined she would've have drifted over to the other side. She leaned forward until her forehead touched the marble floor. When she sat back up, she told them to close their eyes. Peter did and began to look inside himself—a strange but wonderful feeling. It was not frightening, as Peter had always thought it would be. He realized whatever he was going to find there was simply more of him.

The three of them sat with their eyes closed. The smell of the incense, the chanting of the monks served to push them into a place where they were lost beyond space and time. Peter didn't realize how deep he had gone until he heard Pen's voice, which seemed to come from another room. He turned and looked into her eyes. "Now I have Him," she smiled. Then she turned and looked the other way at Kate who, spellbound by her beauty, lifted Pen's arm and kissed it. When Kate and Peter both stood up to go, Pen, with sadness in her eyes, said, "I want to be with Him longer—is it okay?"

"We'll wait for you outside," Peter said. Then he and Kate walked out into the white light. When Pen emerged a few minutes later, the three of them embraced. A young girl speaking with an Australian accent stood with her mother staring up in awe at the sparkling building. "Oh Mommy, it's just like Christmas!"

Her mother glared at the two Westerners together with a Thai girl—obviously appalled. "No, Cynthia, this is Buddhism," she told her daughter, "It's a religion very different from what we believe."

Mr. Kim, relaxing on the stucco wall by the sampan, slightly round and quite wise about the ways of the world, looked like a worldly Buddha himself. Sliding down off the wall as they approached, he told them, "Ahhh, I see Buddha have good effect!"

They followed him back to the sampan and headed off into the harbor back toward downtown Bangkok.

46

Peter stood, in only his olive drab underpants, on the raised platform in the tailor shop. Kate, Pen, and Mr. Kim sat in comfortable chairs drinking cool Tiger beers. They were the audience for the fitting. The tailor raced with his assistant in tow out of the back room carrying five or six different-colored bolts of silk, which they set on the platform. The tailor, who was obviously used to working very quickly, hastily unrolled a white bolt, wrapping it around Peter's waist then over his shoulders. Peter, looking like a monk, brought his palms to his forehead and closed his eyes. When he brought his palms back down, the tailor's assistant slipped a cool Tiger beer between his hands.

"My prayers are answered."

"You pray for beer?" asked Mr. Kim.

"I pray for peace."

Mr. Kim got off his seat and whispered into the tailor's ear. The tailor then ran off to the back room and emerged with a roll of saffron-colored silk. Peter had a mouthful of beer and almost choked when he saw the fabric. "That's it!"

"Don't I tell you?" Mr. Kim smiled at the tailor, who wrapped Peter in the silk, tucking it expertly at the waist, as a monk would tie it.

"Just what you always wanted, Peter," Kate laughed, "only it needs pockets . . ."

"Now for Miss White." Peter pulled Kate up onto the platform.

"No, Pen first." Kate pulled her by the arm up onto the platform. "You must undress first," Kate whispered in her ear.

Pen unabashedly pulled her dress over her head. She wore nothing underneath. Peter and Kate both relished looking at her. Kate stepped out of her dress and her panties. She ran her fingers down Pen's back. Kate enjoyed standing naked with Pen so much that it almost hurt when the tailor's assistant began wrapping Pen's body in yellow silk.

The tailor wrapped Kate in emerald green. When he was done, he placed a Thai-style conical hat on her head. She looked stunning.

"Beautiful," said Mr. Kim.

"Yes." Peter looked into Kate's eyes. He reached for her hand and walked both women out the door into the busy street. Mr. Kim ran after them, running to his car to hold the door open.

"Back to the temple?" he asked.

"To the temple of love," Peter said mischievously.

"Ahhh," said Mr. Kim. "Siam."

47

Under the hot red lights in the steam room at the Siam, Kate turned in slow circles as Peter tugged on the end of the long piece of green silk. Soft Thai music filtered through a speaker in the ceiling and echoed off the black stone walls. With each turn Peter placed a kiss on Kate's mouth. He turned her until all the silk was undone and had fallen to the floor. They continued to kiss while Kate slowly unwound Peter's long piece of silk. Clouds of steam wafted through the room. Red heat lamps made it seem as if the two lovers had fallen into an ancient volcano that had begun to erupt around them. Weak with passion, they fell to the hot stone floor caressing each other's bodies. Beads of sweat became rivers flowing down their skin. Peter licked the sweat from Kate's neck, then from her upper lip. "Hotter than Vietnam," he said. He licked the river that flowed between her breasts and ran down her stomach between her legs.

"Hotter than hell," she said, when he looked up into her eyes. She leaned to lick the sweat from his shoulder.

"Salt."

He kissed her breasts.

"Sugar."

Kneeling between her legs he followed the river again down her stomach. Kate placed her hands on his shoulders. She pulled him into her where the river ended. Then Peter lay on top, pressing himself inside her.

Pen entered the room carrying a small brass pot of rose water, which she set on the floor beside the lovers. Pen lovingly ladled the water over Kate and Peter as they made love. Peter lifted himself off and Pen leaned down. Kate, looking deep into Pen's eyes, kissed her full on the mouth. "Spice," Kate whispered.

48

Kate leaned against Peter on the familiar seat on the open deck of a Huey that snaked along the Song Tra Bong. It was a stormy, overcast day and they were the only passengers. As the two of them stared blankly down at the green of Vietnam, Peter remembered his first flight out to Camp Fort Lauderdale with Marcus. Then, quickly, he pushed the thought from his mind. Peter was thinking how tired he had become of the green of the jungle. He had seen too much of it and for too long. Looking down at the green blur made him begin to feel sick to his stomach.

The farther downriver they went, the more evident were the signs of the war's devastation—bomb craters and scorched earth and the black skeletons of trees burned to a crisp by napalm. As the chopper followed a sharp turn in the river, their eyes fell on a huge crater filled with people. Looking like a painting by Hieronymus Bosch, it was an odd and eerie sight that disturbed them deeply.

Farther on, three or four Vietnamese walked along a dike between two rice paddies. Suddenly, they were over Camp Fort Lauderdale. From the air, the camp was a sprawling city of tents—row upon row—surrounded on all sides by a perimeter of concertina wire and sandbagged guard posts. It resembled a prison—as if the concertina wire was being used more to keep the detainees in than to keep the enemy out.

The chopper settled down into the clearing where Marcus and Peter had first met Broward. Peter jumped down as soon as the chopper hit the grass. Kate followed him down an alley between two tent rows. They wanted to disappear as quickly as they could, before Broward knew they had come.

"We need to find the village chief, Van Binh," Peter spoke across his shoulder to Kate. A young Vietnamese boy who had been following them said, "I take you Van Binh," figuring he'd make a few piasters for his trouble. By the time they reached Van Binh's tent, there were thirty or more children following, hoping for some money, or at least to have their pictures taken.

Than Van Binh was unusually rotund for a Vietnamese. He had a head of pure white hair and a small goatee that came to a point under his chin, making him look surprisingly like Ho Chi Minh. He sat alone in his tent, cross-legged, regal on an Oriental carpet with a small writing board balanced on his knees—a symbol of education. When Kate and Peter entered his tent he was writing a letter with a fine French fountain pen. He took his royal time before bothering to acknowledge them. When he finally looked up, the two reporters greeted him placing their palms together, bringing them to their foreheads, bowing. Kate handed the village chief a carton of Salems. Van Binh looked pleased.

"*Chao ong,*" Peter said. "We are correspondents, reporters. We're here to write about the refugees and we need your help."

Van Binh looked interested in something else. He pointed to Peter's camera. "*Chao ong.*"

Lifting the camera strap over his head, Peter handed him his Pentax.

Kate, as always, got right to the point. "Can you tell us about the crater where people are being held?"

Van Binh struggled with the focus, unwittingly shooting a picture of Peter. "You take me," he handed the camera back to Peter, smoothly avoiding Kate's question.

Kate took a few shots of the village chief with her Nikon before Van Binh covered his face, obviously not wanting to deal with a woman.

Peter took his picture, asking him at the same time, "What about your people who can't live in Fort Lauderdale? Where are they? What will you do for them, Van Binh?"

The chief disregarded Peter's question and asked instead, "My picture in *Playboy?*"

"Yes, Van Binh, you be centerfold," Peter said sarcastically.

Both Kate and Peter knew that Vietnamese who held positions of power liked to play games of deflection. The game was to avoid the opponent's point.

The village chief burst out laughing, putting out his hands a foot from his chest. "Van Binh, centerfold!"

Peter knew that with Van Binh, they would have to resort to the currency that seemed to work with any Vietnamese, no matter what their status. He reached into his shirt pocket and pulled out a brand-new polished brass Zippo lighter. Offering Van Binh a Camel, he lit it for him, holding the lighter in front of his face for longer than usual. He wanted Van Binh to have a good look at it. Peter turned to Kate. "Ask him your question," he said, flipping the top of the lighter closed and placing it in Van Binh's small hand.

Kate began, "Van Binh, Fort Lauderdale holds only a few thousand of your people. Where are the fifty thousand others? What happened to them?"

Van Binh smiled, expertly flicking open the top to his new lighter. "Yes, this camp, only a few thousand . . . but everybody . . ." Suddenly his unusually jovial expression turned serious, sad. "Homes gone . . . villages gone . . . everything lost . . . farms, cattle. Operation Browar' County very bad for South Vietnamese. Thousands with no home."

"Where are these people?" Kate pressed him further, furiously scribbling notes in her small spiral notebook.

"Many die . . . without food. Operation destroy rice crop. Monsoon rain kill many. No homes. No fire to keep warm. Many die from cold . . ." His voice trailed off sadly.

"Do you know about the big crater by the river?" she asked. Van Binh looked up into her eyes but didn't answer.

Jake Broward's ugly voice suddenly ricocheted between the tents outside. "How the hell did they get in? Where are they? Oh shit, don't tell me—not with Van Binh!"

Perfectly timed for the moment Broward's huge red face pushed through the flap in the tent, Van Binh said, "No, thank you," handing the carton of Salems back to Kate. "Not the brand I smoke." He swiftly slipped the lighter beneath his leg.

The colonel had fire in his eyes. "Who let you into my camp without my permission?"

Then Peter watched as the look in his eyes softened and he changed his tack. His voice turned almost melodious. "Miss White, Sergeant Hill—come to write a story about Fort Lauderdale?"

Peter offered a proper salute, "Afternoon, sir. Very impressive, sir," Peter feigned interest, "what you're doing here."

Peter was surprised to see his former interpreter, Lan, follow Zippo into the tent.

"You've outdone yourself," Kate said to Broward.

"Yes, well, with Fort Lauderdale we are showing a new American face to the Vietnamese . . ." He paused. "Say, aren't you going to write this down, Miss White?"

Kate lifted her notebook. "You certainly are a man of many faces, Colonel," she said sardonically.

Broward, happy that Kate was writing, let the remark pass. "We have taken in more than six thousand refugees," he lied, "who are being fed three hot meals a day. We're teaching the Vietnamese the *American Way* here at Fort Lauderdale. We've set up a free enterprise system to supply them with all the necessities—toothpaste, shampoo . . . my God," he grinned at Kate, "we even sell them Tampax, don't we, Lieutenant?"

"Tampax. Yes, sir!"

"We show them a different movie every night . . . Zippo, what's the . . ."

"*The Graduate*, sir."

Broward frowned, "What's that—a skin flick?"

"It's a big hit back home, sir."

The colonel beamed widely at Kate and Peter. "You will be my guests for dinner and a movie tonight."

"We're expected back in Chu Lai, sir," Peter told him.

"We'll have plenty of time to talk over some juicy steaks. You came to get a story, didn't you?"

"Sir . . ."

Broward cut him off. But Peter didn't want to argue, feeling they were closing in on the missing facts that could incriminate Broward beyond a doubt.

"You two feel free to wander around and take whatever pictures you want. We'll meet at my tent at nineteen hundred for chow. Lieutenant Zippo will escort you until then . . ." Broward swiveled his huge barrel of a body abruptly and stormed out through the tent flaps, flashing an angry look at Van Binh before he went. Lan and Zippo followed like baby ducks after their mother.

Zippo, Kate, and Peter stood together, letting Broward's wake settle for a moment.

"What can I show you boys and girls?" Zippo spoke in his irritatingly high-pitched voice.

"First off, I need to use the facilities." Peter winked at Kate as they followed the idiotic lieutenant along the tent row.

"Yes, me too," Kate grinned.

Peter knew the shitter was the only place they could talk in private.

Zippo muttered something about what a fine sanitation system they had built at Fort Lauderdale. "Dumb gooks have to be trained to shit into the hole," he added. "Can't even aim straight!"

"No lessons necessary here," Peter said, stepping into the long ply-wood shack.

Kate followed him in, a spring slamming the door behind her.

Zippo lit up a smoke and politely turned his back.

"I actually do have to pee," she grinned at Peter, pulling her pants down as the two of them sat side by side.

"Listen, the only way we're ever going to lose Zippo is down through the shitter and out the back," Peter whispered to her.

Kate stood and quietly buttoned up her pants. Peter lifted the hinged piece of plywood they'd been sitting on and they lowered themselves down into the shithole trying their best not to step into one of the cut-off fifty-five-gallon drums that sat beneath each hole. Though the cans were filled with diesel fuel, they still gave off a horrible stench.

One of Kate's feet slipped into the can below her when she low-ered herself. Peter poured some diesel from a jerry can over her boot to kill the smell. Then they sneaked off along the tent row behind the shitter and headed toward the perimeter of the camp. Reaching the end of the row, they surprised, atop a sandbagged bunker, a guard post of ARVNs, who were in the process of sharing a large joint. They com-ically tried to hide it from view.

"Smokin' a Salem, eh?" Peter said in a serious tone. "You know the punishment for smoking marijuana on guard duty. Show us the way out and we won't tell Broward."

One of the soldiers jumped down quickly and helped them through a small break in the wire.

"You go first," Peter told him. "Take us to the crater," he ordered, knowing the soldier would steer them clear of mines outside the perime-ter. They headed across a narrow dike separating the rice paddies. When they reached the other side, the soldier pointed down a path continuing through some trees. "Just a hundred meters," he said. "On other side." Peter handed the Vietnamese soldier the carton of Salems he'd brought for Van Binh. "Smoke these, they might save your life."

Ominously, the sky was becoming dark as Peter lead the way down the narrow path. A light rain began to fall. He stopped and looked back at Kate. They heard horrible screams coming from the clearing beyond the trees. Peter cautiously moved ahead a few more meters until he found himself standing right behind a South Vietnamese guard with an M-16 hanging at his side. Peter grabbed the guard around the neck and pulled him backward onto the ground. He dragged him back into the underbrush, holding the barrel of his M-16 to his throat. "Who do you work for?" Peter glared into his eyes.

"Me, ARVN—guard prisoners," he answered, terrified.

Peter spoke through clenched teeth. "You VC motherfucker—yes?" he said, scaring him into telling the truth.

"Me work Colonel Browar'," he admitted. "I take you to Lieutenant Than."

Peter, unable to control his mounting anger, clocked the soldier in the side of the head with the stock of his M-16.

Kate was surprised at the depth of Peter's sudden anger for a Vietnamese, even a South Vietnamese. It was nothing she hadn't witnessed before—just not with Peter. She followed him into the clearing. On the far side they saw the crater. Coming from inside the huge hole they heard painful screams of mothers crying for food for their children. The sounds were horrible. They both attracted and repelled at the same time, making them first want to look then suddenly turn around and flee. Peter felt like he didn't want to witness the horror—he'd seen enough in the last few weeks to last a lifetime. But he realized that like Kate, he too was a reporter, and it was his duty to help her get the story.

It was at that moment, hearing the horrific cries for help from other human beings, that Peter knew he'd changed. For the first time, he saw himself as a correspondent in the larger sense of the word. He knew he would have to write the story as it was—not just as the army would publish it. He knew his duty was to the people in the crater. They were not the enemy—they were South Vietnamese, the people they'd come to protect. But more than that, they were just people.

The screaming drew them closer, but as they approached the crater the sounds were almost unbearable. Neither of them was prepared for what they saw when they reached the edge. It was far worse than they could have imagined. On the ground, the crater was bigger than it had looked from the air—about fifty meters across. The bottom was flooded with water and there was room for less than half the people on the small islands that remained above the waterline. There were hundreds of Vietnamese in the bunker—old men, and women with their children. Many sat up to their waists in cold water, clinging to each other for warmth. The people had no protection from the rain and cold. Many had died from exposure. It was hard to tell who was alive and who had already died.

Kate was so disturbed by the sight she could hardly move. She knew she had to get photographs so she panned her camera back and forth across the people, taking shot after shot. She looked as though she was about to faint. Her face turned white.

A chill of fear ran up Peter's spine when he suddenly thought of Broward. Peter knew the crater would be the one place Broward would not want them to see. When he found they had given Zippo the slip, it would not be long before the colonel would come looking. Peter kept his M-16 at the ready, covering Kate while she shot a second roll of film.

Three Vietnamese Popular Force guards were posted around the rim. They watched Kate and Peter suspiciously but, thinking they surely must have had the colonel's permission to be there, didn't prevent them from taking pictures.

The man in charge, ARVN Lieutenant Than, finally emerged from a small guardhouse, looking haggard and undernourished himself. Peter immediately walked toward him to distract him from seeing Kate taking pictures. "Are you in charge here, Lieutenant? These people are dying, Lieutenant. They're starving."

"We radio for food." He nearly wept when he spoke. "No food for three days . . ."

"You're right next to Fort Lauderdale!"

"They tell me food is coming . . ."

"Why are these people here?" Peter pressed him, feeling like the reporter he'd imagined himself to be back at Yale.

"Too old, too sick—can't work."

Peter followed the lieutenant's eyes as they surveyed the area. His eyes seemed to show that he was about to reveal something important.

"What kind of work do you mean?"

"Work on Broward's plantation."

"What?"

"Cut cinnamon bark."

The sound of a helicopter taking off from Fort Lauderdale echoed through the trees behind them.

"Where's the cinnamon plantation?" Peter raised his voice, pressing the lieutenant to answer quickly, knowing they were out of time—that the chopper would be delivering Broward.

The lieutenant, with fear in his eyes, told him, "West of Quang Ngai—highway to Kontum." Peter knew the Vietnamese soldier wanted, down deep, to betray Broward. It was obvious the young man had seen how poorly the ugly American treated his people.

Colonel Broward's command helicopter swooped in above them, landing beside the crater. The prop wash blew the hats of the people in the hole and scattered whatever they weren't clinging to.

Colonel Broward jumped down from the chopper, followed by Lieutenant Zippo and Lan. As they marched toward them, all hell broke loose. The chopper had attracted the attention of the NVA. Eight or ten AK-47 rifles suddenly opened fire from across the river. Everyone hit the ground. Broward yelled, "Get me the radio, Zippo. We'll call in artillery on the sons-of-bitches!" Zippo ran to the chopper, returning with a heavy PRC-25 radio. Broward kneeled on the ground beside it, obviously struggling with the dials. "Find me the frequency, Zippo! Get me the fort!" Zippo held out the handset for Broward, who tried to find the position on the map. "What are the goddamn coordinates? One, five, three . . ." he called into the headset.

A barrage of NVA bullets danced across the turf beside the colonel. As Kate changed the film in her camera, Peter pulled her away from the crater. He pushed her to the ground when he heard an artillery shell whistling overhead. A huge explosion shattered the air as the first shell hit the side of the crater. The ground itself seemed to groan. Awful, sickening screams came from the people in the hole. A second shell hit just past the rim on the far side.

"Hold fire, goddamnit!" Broward yelled into the radio.

Kate lifted her Nikon. When Broward saw what she was doing, his face went red with rage. "Kill her!" Broward yelled.

Peter lifted his M-16, aiming it directly at Broward's head. He tugged at Kate's sleeve with his free hand but she wouldn't budge. She was fixated on what she saw inside the crater. There were people with arms and legs blown off—still alive and screaming. Kate kneeled at the edge of the hole, pointing her camera into the crater, but she had to look away, unable to watch the horror any longer. She let the camera's motor drive run through the remainder of the film.

Another barrage of NVA fire came from across the river. Peter pulled Kate by the arm.

Slowly he backed her away from Broward, his M-16 still aimed directly at his chest. Peter wanted to pull the trigger but didn't.

"He's got to kill us now," Kate said.

"We have to run for the river," Peter told her, keeping his eyes on Broward.

Kate turned. Then, at that moment, Peter heard a single shot ring out.

Peter hadn't noticed Lan standing off to one side. It was he who shot Kate.

Kate fell to the ground. Peter dived down beside her. He watched a pool of blood form in her hair. He pressed his hand on the wound to stop the bleeding but blood spurted between his fingers. Then he pressed his bloody hand against her neck and felt no pulse. He couldn't believe Kate was dead.

A string of bullets from the NVA across the river buried themselves in the mud beside him. He turned and fired back until the magazine was empty. His head was spinning—he was dazed and dizzy. He lifted Kate's head off the ground, pulling her camera strap over it. He didn't know which way to go—there were enemies in both directions. Putting the camera strap over his head, he ran toward the river.

He didn't stop at the riverbank; he jumped straight into the rapid current of the pitch-black river. *Kate is dead,* he kept thinking. There was little coherent thought left in his brain—his normal thinking process shut down. He was on automatic, his brain cells rapid-firing, helping him do what he needed to do. Holding his breath, he remained underwater for as long as he could.

Oddly, he thought of the first time he'd held his breath underwater. He was five and it was his first swimming lesson. Strangely enough, it was in the pool at Pine Crest Country Day School, in Fort Lauderdale, Florida.

When he was forced to come up for air he found himself only about one-third of the way across the river. He thought of continuing across to the other side, then he remembered the NVA. He dunked under again, deciding to let the current take him downstream. When he came to the surface again, he saw that the sky was nearly dark and the shooting had stopped. He had drifted out of harm's way. He thought, for safety's sake, he would let the river continue to carry him farther before he swam to shore.

As he drifted downstream all Peter could think about was Kate. Part of him wanted to go back to see her again—just to hold her one more time. He even thought of bringing her body back down the river with him. Her death hadn't hit him yet. He was thinking about Marcus too, and Catchahorse and Sullivan and even Spellbinder. It seemed he was leaving a trail of dead bodies behind him. Kate was the last in line.

49

Within a few minutes all daylight was gone. Peter thought he would be safe beneath the cover of darkness until he saw Broward's Huey hovering ten meters above the river, its searchlight ominously sweeping back and forth across the surface of the water. Caught in the current, he was moving helplessly closer to the bright red tracer rounds coming from the door gunners, who were churning the water into foam with their M-60 machine guns. Then when the chopper was about twenty meters in front of him, the NVA on the far bank opened up on the chopper, shooting out its searchlight. As Peter floated under the Huey, the guns went silent and the chopper headed off blindly for the protection of the open sky.

Peter let the current take him a few miles farther downstream—until he felt he was safely beyond the North Vietnamese troops. Freezing cold, he swam to the far bank in the dark, crashing headlong into a tree that had fallen into the river. With the current pinning him against it, it took every ounce of strength to pull himself out of the water. He rested for a minute then crawled along the trunk to the riverbank. Reaching the shore, he turned onto his back to rest, completely exhausted, unable to move another inch. He let his head fall back onto the grass.

Then he felt the cold steel of a muzzle against his forehead.

"*Dung lai!*" a deep American-sounding voice followed down the gun barrel.

A hand reached out of the dark, grabbing him by the hair, lifting his head off the ground. A bright light shot directly into his brain. Peter turned his head to escape the pain from the light.

"*Fuck*—you're one of us!" said the voice from behind the light. "Who the fuck are you? Where the fuck did you come from?"

"Upstream," Peter said. He barely had enough energy to speak to the soldier standing over him.

"We heard firing upriver, then saw you floating in the water. We figured you to be a fucking NVA. This place is crawling with Charlie. You're a goddamn lucky dude we didn't shoot."

"Can you get me to Chu Lai?"

50

Peter, wet and as exhausted as he'd ever been, stood at the correspondents' phone in the Americal PIO. He had Randall Guest on
the line. "Yes, that's correct—the wrong coordinates. There were hundreds of Vietnamese in the crater. Not many survived . . ."

Peter hadn't yet mentioned Kate when he heard a commotion at the
far end of the PIO office, followed shortly after by Broward's voice.

"Randy, I gotta go." He hung up.

Broward stormed up to Peter, who stepped away from the phone and
faced him directly. Peter went for his gun, his hand just reaching his holster when he saw Broward's .45 pointed between his eyes. He could almost feel a bullet swimming around in his brain.

He stared into Broward's eyes. "You're too late, Colonel. UPI has the
story." He smiled a satisfied smile.

Broward grabbed for Kate's camera, which still hung from Peter's
neck. As he struggled to pull it off, Peter told him, "The photos are on
their way to UPI by courier. The camera's just a souvenir, Colonel."

Zippo aimed his .45 at Peter's forehead. "Say the word, sir."

"The word is *fucked*," Broward shouted at Zippo, a spray of spit hitting him in the face. "We're fucked, you asshole!" Broward turned his gun
on his lieutenant.

Zippo couldn't contain himself. From only a few feet away, Peter saw him begin to squeeze the trigger anyway. Peter watched Zippo's skull shatter and his body slither down the front of a filing cabinet, his idiot grin gone forever.

Peter felt a stinging sensation in his shoulder. He peered down and saw the small hole in his shirt where Zippo's bullet had hit him. Weakened, he found himself on the floor struggling to lift his .45. He pointed it at Broward and pulled the trigger. Broward appeared for a moment as if he was about to settle in and read the Sunday papers—except for the river of blood that gushed from his chest. He reeled, then slowly settled back into a canvas chair looking down at his chest at something he'd never even considered—his own mortality.

Peter tried to lift his head but found he couldn't. Finally, succumbing to the exhaustion that seemed to be settling over his body like a blanket, he laid the back of his head down on the floor. For some reason, the last thing he remembered before drifting off was searching the room for Kate.

51

The bright, early-morning sun poured through the window in Gisella's office. Peter took a sip of Dunkin' Donuts coffee before setting the paper cup on the coffee table. "All I know is . . . I didn't want to see . . . any more death . . ." His words seemed to fade slowly away toward silence. He closed his eyes, watching tiny beads of light drift across the blackness behind his eyelids. Finally he opened them again and stared down at the floor.

"When I was on the phone with Randy, I couldn't tell him Kate had been killed." Peter paused to drink some coffee, finding the words were hard in coming. "There were certain things you didn't want to say. You didn't want to talk about death. It wasn't just me, nobody did. I didn't want to talk about Kate. I didn't want to tell Randy . . ." Peter drifted off again.

Gisella chose not to speak. Instead, she waited patiently.

When Peter surfaced, he was more intense. "Gisella, I can help you. I can help you understand something. Something you can use to help the other fucked-up Vietnam vets—hell, vets from any fucking war."

Peter heard Gisella's voice as if it came from a great distance. "I'd like to know."

"Yes . . . of course . . . you'd like to know," he replied, angrily. "Well, I can fucking tell you what war is all about."

"Tell me," Gisella said, softly, gently.

"It's about death." He looked up at her, to make sure she'd heard. When he was certain, he went on. "It's really very simple. Wise men have all these commentaries about what war is about—power struggles and religious beliefs and occupying land. All bullshit. And, getting closer to the facts here, war is not about killing. It's only about one thing—it's about death and dying."

Peter sank into the couch. It comforted him. He knew that for once, he'd said something worthwhile. Although he'd already made his point, he went on for emphasis. He was on a roll. "I know, because I was there, Gisella. It's not what you see on TV and it's not what you read in books. All these books you've read—all the reasons they give—they're all wrong. Did you ever see one of those movies about the Civil War when five hundred soldiers line up in a long line and face five hundred enemy soldiers in another long line and they begin shooting and men begin to fall down and you see actors moaning and writhing around on the ground? Or when the guy in a World War II movie gets shot and puts his hand over his heart, some blood spurts out, and then he falls back on his ass? Why does it always look fake? No movie director ever made it look real. And why can't they make it look real? Because when someone dies in a war, you can't see it. You can't tell when he dies. Like the guy on the floor of the chopper when Kate and I were flying back from the A Shau— what was dramatic about that? Nothing. Not a fucking thing. You never even knew that the guy had died. You didn't *see* him die, for chrissakes! Even if you were looking you didn't see it. Because you can't fucking *see* death! But that's what it's all about. It's about a bunch of fucked-up guys who think they can fool death, but can't. It always fools them instead. It finds them. It catches them when they're not looking."

When Peter had finished, he looked up at Gisella. He noticed her face had turned pale.

"I'm afraid we are out of time for today, Peter," she said softly.

52

Peter waited in front of the closed door of the Buddhist temple near Tam Ky. He was not seeing the door; instead he was lost somewhere inside his head. When he felt ready to go in, he pulled open the door. The cool air from inside seemed to invite him in. The sound of his heavy boots echoed loudly off the temple walls. As his eyes adjusted to the dim light, he saw a young Buddhist monk sitting on the floor reading from a large book in his lap. Stepping self-consciously around the monk, making sure not to disturb him, Peter walked toward the altar at the far end.

The powerful silence in the temple seemed to stop him in the middle of the room, and he sat down on the floor facing the statue of Buddha. Sitting on the cold floor, exhausted, he became conscious of his own breathing. It seemed far too heavy for the subtle place.

He set down his M-16 on the floor, looking at the battered black shape of the automatic weapon that had been through so much with him. But it was as if he was beginning to see it for what it was. In his head, though he'd never said it out loud, Peter had named his gun Maybelline, after the Chuck Berry tune. Peter had come to the temple to surrender and his M-16 was the first thing in his possession he thought of surrendering. *Oh no—not Maybelline*, he thought. What would happen if the temple was attacked? Maybe it wasn't time to let her go. He convinced himself she was not yet ready to leave. Okay. He would hold on to her for a while.

He lay down on the floor, greatly relieved to be where he was, flat on his back within the safety of the temple walls, looking up at the ceiling.

His mind raced, filled with thoughts of the war. But then, in spite of himself, he began to contemplate the color blue on the ceiling. Even in the dim light, the color remained bright—a good approximation of a clear blue sky, which reminded him of a painting by the Italian Renaissance painter Tiepolo hanging in the Yale Museum of Art. He realized that the ceiling was exactly the same color as Tiepolo's sky. He'd heard a lecturer call it "cerulean blue."

At first, the silence surrounding him allowed his mind to begin to quiet itself. His thoughts settled down. But then something strange happened—as soon as his mind began to empty itself of thoughts, it would instantly begin to fill up again with an entirely new stream. He tried not to think—but only to notice. He saw that the light from outside filtered into the temple through an ornate metal grate above the altar, creating a pattern of flower petals on the wall.

This didn't work at all. Noticing involved thinking. He decided not to worry about thoughts, about thinking, about noticing. Then suddenly it was easier.

He moved his eyes around the temple. He saw that among the faded symbols on the walls, a swastika had been painted above the doorway. Although Peter knew it was an ancient Buddhist symbol, it reminded him of Hitler and the Nazis. Once he had known why Hitler had picked the symbol but now he'd forgotten. Then he thought, it was the Americans who were the Nazis in this war he was in. The Americans with their gigantic machines of destruction—the huge twin-engine Chinook helicopters, gunships, tanks, even. Tanks appeared so odd and out of place in Vietnam. There was no place for tanks there in the highlands. Tanks wouldn't be able to move in the dense jungle or up the steep mountainsides. The tanks must be in Saigon, he thought, patrolling the city streets. Blasting the brothels. He imagined American tanks roaring through the streets of Saigon, crushing buildings, squishing people like overripe melons, heads popping, eyes popping. On the sides of the tanks swastikas were painted just above the words UNITED STATES ARMY. He imagined John Wayne playing the part of Hitler in the German version of *The Green Berets*.

Peter turned angry. Why, in these beautiful and quiet surroundings, he thought, did he need to think about tanks, about Hitler—about war at all? He had come to the temple to escape these things and they had followed him.

He turned to look at the monk, who was still engaged in the book in his lap. "Where am I?" he asked, his voice echoing in the room much louder than he imagined it would.

The monk continued to read, not even bothering to acknowledge Peter. Peter grew angry but held himself in check and decided not to repeat his question. He thought the monk may have had a reason for not answering. Peter turned and faced the altar again, noticing that the small statue of Buddha was staring directly down at him. The look in Buddha's eyes was oddly powerful, painted with a blue outline around them. The eyes were not almond-shaped, but resembled a wave. In the center, the irises were filled with gold, which seemed to give them the power to pierce right through him.

He heard the monk speak softly, in perfect English from behind him. "No answer is also an answer."

Again Peter turned to look at the monk, but he had gone back to reading his book. He decided he would try to ignore him. After all, Peter had come to surrender, which had nothing to do with the monk. He decided that the temple, as small as it was, was big enough for the both of them.

He began to unlace his boots. He pulled them off and placed them side by side beneath the statue of Buddha. He surrendered his boots.

Peter turned to see if the monk was watching. Instead he noticed his M-16 sitting in the middle of the temple floor. He realized it was

now closer to the monk than to him. If he had wanted to, Peter
thought, the monk could easily reach it first. Turning back toward the
altar, he realized that he didn't care if the monk wanted to shoot him
or not. The monk could race over to Maybelline, load her up with a
magazine, and turn him into Swiss cheese for all Peter cared. He no
longer gave a holy shit.

Peter went back to what he was doing. He pulled his socks off,
folding them just as he'd learned in basic training, placing them neatly
across the toes of the boots.

He stood up, feeling the weight of the two canteens hanging from
his web belt. He unbuckled the canteens and placed them on the altar,
one on either side of the boots. He surrendered his canteens. Then he
removed his wallet from the breast pocket of his shirt and set it down
on the floor. He undid his fatigue shirt, button by button, pulling it off,
folding it before laying it neatly on the altar. Immediately Peter realized he felt less tied to the world. Lighter.

He unbuttoned his pants, which quickly dropped to the from the
weight of all he carried in the pockets. He stepped out of his pants and
undershorts then bent down to remove two cans of C rations from the
cargo pockets. One spaghetti and meatballs, one peanut butter and
crackers. He emptied out the remaining contents of his pant pockets: two
pens, his notebook, waterproof matches, a pack of Camels, a flashlight.
Again, as he had been taught to do in basic training, he folded the pants,
carefully placing them in a neat pile on the altar. He felt even better.

He sat down again on the cold floor, a shiver running straight up his
spine. His cheeks contracted from the cold. He emptied the contents of
his wallet onto the floor: Geneva Convention card. Rogers Raiders card.
Rifle Cleaning Tips. Booby Trap Awareness card. Connecticut driver's license. Forty-three Vietnamese piasters. Seven dollars Military Payment
Certificates. Picture of his family. Picture of Jesus. Military Shot Record.
Draft card. Social Security card. Spare pack of matches—waterproof.
One dime. Picture of himself in front of his 1960 yellow Ford station
wagon back in Connecticut.

He picked up the Booby Trap Awareness card and began to read it.
"Mines and booby traps can kill, so be alert—stay alive."
He thought of Sullivan.
"If possible, don't be in too much of a hurry. Never take anything for granted, it might look harmless but it might be a killer."
He thought of Broward and put the card down. Then he unfolded a yellowed piece of paper. The title at the top read: OPERATOR PREVENTIVE MAINTENANCE CHECKLIST FOR M-16-A1 RIFLE. It reminded him of the poem by Henry Reed, "Naming of Parts," which he'd read in Joe Rice's class. He and Marcus had sat together in the back row. Michael Conforti sat next to them. Peter began to read it as if it were a poem:

> THE UPPER RECEIVER GROUP:
> Barrel exterior is clean and lightly oiled.
> Front sight post is free to move and is properly
>   lubricated.
> Bayonet stud will accept and hold bayonet in place.
> Front sling swivel is firmly attached and free of rust.
> Gas tube is firmly attached and free of dents or bends.
> Slip ring spring is firm, clean, and properly lubricated.
> Windage knob moves freely, is free of rust and is
>   properly lubricated.
> Windage knob detent works freely, holds windage in
>   selected position, is free of rust and is properly
>   lubricated.
> Locking lugs are clean and lightly oiled.
> Gas tube extension inside upper receiver is clean and
>   dry.
> Inside of upper receiver is clean and dry . . .

He remembered what he could of Henry Reed's poem—the first verse—which he recited out loud:

Today we have the naming of parts.
Yesterday we had daily cleaning.
And tomorrow morning, We shall have to do after
    firing.
Japonica glistens like coral in all of the neighboring
    gardens,
And today we have naming of parts.

Peter noticed the monk had looked up from his book. So he picked up another card off the floor and read the title out loud: "The Enemy in Your Hands." He unfolded it and read the inside, "As a member of the U.S. Military Forces, you will comply with the Geneva Prisoner of War Conventions of 1949 to which your country adheres. Under these conventions: You can and will—Disarm your prisoner. Immediately search him thoroughly. Require him to be silent. Segregate him from other prisoners. Guard him carefully in the place designated by your commander. You cannot and must not—Mistreat your prisoner. Humiliate or degrade him. Take any of his personal effects which do not have significant military value. Refuse him medical treatment if required and available. Always treat your prisoner humanely . . ."

Peter thought of the prisoner who had been thrown from a chopper he had ridden in from the field. A couple of South Vietnamese policemen had been unsuccessful in getting the young NVA to talk so they tossed him out the door. One of the policemen grabbed the boy by the head, the other by the feet, and they made him spin as they pushed him out of the helicopter. They could hardly stop laughing. The pilot flew in a circle so everyone could watch the boy spin all the way down to the ground.

53

Peter stared out the window in Gisella's office. He was thinking of the young NVA soldier who had died. The one Marcus and he had flown out to write a story about. The one Broward had wanted his picture taken with. "He was only a boy, just a few years younger than me at the time," Peter said. "I remember, when we went through his wallet we found a picture of him standing in front of his house with his mother and father and sister. And, you know what's really weird, Gisella?"

"Tell me."

"I really think I could've made friends with that guy. I know, that probably sounds strange, since I'd only known him when he was alive for an hour or less. But he seemed like a really nice fellow. Then, when Marcus and I found the picture of him with his family—it's like, for a second, I thought I could've been over at his house having dinner—you know, talking with his parents and his sister. Is that strange?" He looked at Gisella, suddenly feeling a need to connect.

"No, not really," she said.

"What does that mean, 'not really'?"

"Just an expression. No, it doesn't seem strange. You were both teenagers, both soldiers."

"But what were we fighting for? Why the fuck were we there in the

203

first place? The war was so fucking complicated. It was *their* war—not mine. That's what we all found out—we Americans—once we got there. It wasn't our war at all. And . . . the worst part was that *we* kept on fighting even when the South Vietnamese *wouldn't. They* knew who was winning the fucking war!"

"You're right, Peter. We all know that now—years later. After the fact."

"Meanwhile, it fucked a lot of people up. Permanently. The ARVNs stopped fighting while fucking Americans were still dying!"

Peter turned from the window and looked into Gisella's eyes.

"Gisella, have you seen many people die?" he asked.

She appeared surprised. "Why do you ask? Does it make a difference one way or the other?"

"No big deal," he said. "I just wanted to know."

"We're almost out of time. Is there anything . . ."

"Yes. You know what I wish?"

"What?"

"I wish I could have saved that kid's life. Just that one."

54

Peter picked up the contents of his wallet off the temple floor, placing them on a shiny brass tray beneath the statue of Buddha. He tried to light a waterproof match but it fizzled and went out. Then another. On the seventh and last match, the flame caught. Feeling drained and without any sentiment, he set his driver's license on fire. For some reason, his license seemed to carry a heavy weight—perhaps, he thought, because it was the oldest of all the objects in the pile. The license was dry and burned rapidly. He then placed all the other cards on the pile until the fire grew quite large. He dropped the crinkled piasters into the flames, watching them catch fire in a quick burst. How easily money burns, he thought. Easier than anything.

He put the pictures on top last. Peter wanted to kill the memories—all of them—until there were none left. It would be like he was no longer alive. But also he wanted to surrender his memories to a place for safekeeping—to something, someone, anything, bigger than himself—to Buddha.

He no longer wanted his memories to be contained within himself. There was too much shame involved. Too much guilt. Too much loss. After all, he'd let his best friend die. He'd let the woman he loved die. So there was no way he wanted to be entrusted to hold his family in his head. He didn't want them to die too. He dropped them all into the flame, praying that the memories would be burned up in the flames.

Peter felt like crying but he held back the tears. Only Maybelline, his trusty M-16, and his bandoleer of ammunition remained. The bandoleer contained seven magazines, each containing eighteen rounds of M-16 ammunition. One by one, he pried the bullets from the magazine, placing them upright like candles along the step beneath the altar. The line eventually stretched the entire width of the altar. The shiny brass looked quite beautiful in the light filtering into the temple.

Maybelline. Tears flowed down his cheeks as he removed her carrying straps. He let her bolt slip forward one last time, placing her on safe. Then he took her down. The barrel. The stock. The bolt return spring. Even her trigger mechanism. Maybelline was dead. He placed her broken pieces upon the altar.

The cool breeze chilled Peter's skin. He looked over and received his first smile from the monk. He smiled back, meekly.

Peter wondered how he should sit. Was there some special position he should be in? Feebly, he tried to bend himself into Buddha's pose.

The young monk stood. Again he smiled at Peter. Suddenly embarrassed by his nakedness, Peter turned his head back toward the altar. He closed his eyes for refuge. His next thought was that the monk was a faggot. He felt ashamed to think that. He compensated by thinking of Kate. He thought of her perfect, round breasts and started to get a hard-on. He felt foolish. He prayed for his mind to be silent. He felt the monk's hand upon his shoulder.

"Sit straight," the monk told him.

Peter with his eyes still closed, obeyed. He knew that if he opened his eyes at that moment he would most likely run from the temple. Then he thought of running up to the altar and assembling Maybelline as fast as he could—about four minutes it would take—slapping in a magazine—and killing the monk.

His mind was going berserk. He wanted to control it. He wondered how he could stop the craziness.

The monk pushed Peter forward, sliding a small pillow under his ass. Peter sat back on the pillow, feeling the dried straw scrunch inside the fabric. Suddenly he was comfortable.

How can I stop these thoughts from coming? he thought to himself.

The monk said, "Think all your thoughts—they will pass."

Then the monk walked to the back of the temple, or out, or somewhere. Peter didn't know where. He could hardly hear his footsteps. Then again, he heard the monk return. He heard the monk's footsteps as he walked over. Then he bent down and put a plate on the floor in front of Peter. On the plate lay a single leaf. Peter stared down at it. Studied it. He looked at it and then looked away, then he looked at the altar. After that, he seemed to be looking at nothing at all. For some reason the leaf was filled with meaning for him. But what it meant he wasn't sure. He couldn't quite put it into words—or make it into a thought. He felt like his mind was going to explode. Finally he heard himself shout out loud in frustration, "I don't get it!" Peter shook his head, "I just don't get it . . ."

"A leaf may not be a leaf. Or it may be anything at all. The leaf is whatever you think it is."

He turned around to look. "What if I think it's just a leaf?"

"Then struggle is gone. When struggle is gone, it does not matter."

"Then the leaf . . . doesn't matter?"

"Yes."

Peter looked down at the leaf. It looked like nothing more than a leaf. Slowly and deliberately he picked it up brought it to his mouth and ate it.

55

Peter lay back on Gisella's couch exhausted from telling his story. Gisella stretched her long legs and bent down to pick up a book from the floor beside her chair. Gingerly, she placed it on the coffee table in front of him.

He sat up, "What's this?"

"It's been out of print for some years," she explained as he took the book from the coffee table.

He stared at the book in his hands, stunned. "Kate wrote this book?"

"It's her story." Then Gisella waited, her face filled with compassion. It was too much for him to take in at first.

". . . but?"

"She wrote the book after the war."

"She wasn't killed . . ." Thoughts raced through his mind like a swarm of bees. "What do I do now?" He stared in disbelief at Kate's picture on the jacket. "All this time, thinking she was dead. God, it's been such a long fucking time . . ."

He lay down on the couch—exhausted. He couldn't move. His body felt as frozen solid as his mind. He was simply stunned. He'd accepted that Kate was dead. He wasn't able to suddenly believe that she wasn't. But there on the coffee table was the proof. He held the book up and started to read the blurb on the back. "Back from the dead . . ." it began. He dropped the book on the floor.

"I don't get it, Gisella. I felt her pulse. She was dead—she was gone. There was a bullet hole in her head. My God . . . she was dead! She's not dead."

Peter sat up and looked over at Gisella. "Why didn't you tell me . . . before?"

"I just found out, Peter. I saw her book in a newsletter of Vietnam literature. I sent for her book this week. I couldn't believe it myself."

"This is all so unreal."

"It's real, Peter. It's right there on the table."

Peter turned his head toward the window. "If it's true, why didn't she contact me?"

"You'll have to decide"—Gisella crossed her legs—"what you might want to do."

"Yes," he replied, thinking her words sounded so insignificant—so lame.

Gisella looked at her wristwatch. "We only have a few minutes . . . you'll let me know whatever you decide?"

Gisella walked Peter to the doorway. After opening the door, he answered, "Of course I'll let you know, Gisella. But what should I tell Nina?"

"You'll have to decide."

"I hope she'll understand."

"Do you love her?"

"Nina? Yes."

"Think of how she'll feel . . ."

A storm of conflicting emotions swirled through his head.

56

It was a Sunday morning. It must have been ten or eleven o'clock because the heavy Oregon fog was beginning to burn off. Six of the members of the commune sat together on a huge quilt they'd positioned for the view on the crest of a small hill above the horse meadow. Everyone's eyes followed when a skinny redhead called Buzz stood up and walked over to a tree, where he ran a stick across some ceramic wind chimes hanging from a branch. "Wow," someone said. Everyone on the quilt had eaten two buttons of mescaline. The sound from the wind chime, more crystalline than usual, signaled the drug was taking effect. Their reality was changing. Things were beginning to soften.

Peter sat behind Nina braiding her long hair, which cascaded over her shoulders. He was entranced by the contrast of Nina's light hair, nearly white, with the golden brown color of her skin, which came from living so much out-of-doors.

Nina turned around to smile at Peter. She stood up and led him by the arm down to the white fence, which corralled her two horses, a bay chestnut stallion and a gray-and-white-spotted mare. "You can feed them to gain their trust." She turned Peter's hand palm-up. "Hold it flat," she said, placing two cubes of sugar on it. The mare pushed her head forward, her coarse tongue immediately swiping the cubes off his palm. The stallion kept to the center of the meadow, much too skittish to come near.

Nina ducked between the fence rails, walking up to the stallion, which suddenly appeared gigantic as she approached him. It was obvious she had no fear of him. She grabbed his halter. He shook his head loose and kicked his front legs up above her head. Fearing for her safety, Peter nearly yelled, but as stoned as he was, the instructions from his brain were lost somewhere along the serpentine path to his voice. Peter watched the giant stallion gallop in a circle until suddenly he stopped, dipping his head in submission, and pawed the ground with his front hoof. Nina quickly walked toward him and dived up onto his back. Before she could even sit up, he raced off. He ran directly at Peter with Nina clinging to his mane. Then just when the horse looked as if he was going to jump, he stopped, sending Nina crashing forward against his neck. Anyone less strong than she was would've flown right over the horse's head and over the fence as well. But Nina knew, and more importantly the horse knew, that she had won. Hiking up to her waist the colorful skirt that she had sewn from an Indian bedspread, she turned the horse's head by pulling on his mane, leading him across the meadow in a gallop. The audience on the quilt was transfixed by what they had just witnessed—they had seats at the center ring of the circus.

As Nina circled past, she smiled down over the fence at Peter, like a performer would. Thinking back, he realized the mescaline probably had a lot to do with the feeling that rushed between them. He looked up worshipfully as she rode past on the stallion's back. To him she was more like a medieval goddess than a girl living on a commune. Nina stopped the horse on the far side of the meadow. Peter watched as she pulled her small purple velvet top up over her head. She then pulled her skirt off as well. The next time she rode past Peter, she flung her clothes over the fence. She didn't wear underwear so she was resplendent, he thought, dressed in only her tan—with her blond locks flowing like a flag behind her.

For many years Peter would recount this scene in his mind—at those times when daily life seemed to wear down his marriage to Nina and make her seem mundane. Sometimes, when he grew sick of hearing her voice, he would leave the room and imagine that day. He had done this especially when he'd been drinking. But thinking of Nina that way, naked on the back of the chestnut stallion, always served to rejuvenate his image of her.

When Nina had tired the horse from riding, she pulled up to the fence, her body glistening with sweat. Climbing off, onto the fence, Peter lifted her down, setting her onto the ground, where the two of them made love, stoned, in the grass.

The next morning they packed their few possessions into the Volkswagen van and headed east.

57

Peter and Nina lived with their two young boys in a two-hundred-year-old farmhouse in a valley on the eastern end of East Millbank. Graham was nine, Mathew five. Their house had that lived-in feeling that comes with two energetic boys who thought of walls as places to bounce balls off and furniture as objects to make into forts. There was a lot of art on the walls, mostly pictures painted by the boys, and watercolors Nina had painted in art school, plus some work she had even managed to produce during their marriage. A framed Gauguin print in a simple oak frame hung over the mantel. Nowhere was there any sign of the Far East except for a small brass statue of Buddha used as one half of a set of bookends that held ten or so paperbacks together—mostly Nina's books about childrearing mixed in with a couple of books about Vietnam. *Chickenhawk* was one. *The Things They Carried* was another.

It was dinnertime. Nina stood at the island in the kitchen in front of a large pot of spaghetti onto which she poured some sauce from a saucepan. The kitchen smelled heavily of garlic. Graham was chasing Mathew around the island on Rollerblades. Peter sat at the table in the dining area reading the *East Millbank Crier*.

"Graham!" his mother implored. "How many times have I told you

not to skate in the kitchen? You could knock over the pot and burn
yourself!"

"Rollerblade, Mom! Not *skate*."

Graham was deaf to his mother's words. He made another loop.
Overshooting the kitchen, he careened into the dining table.

"That's it!" Peter yelled, throwing down his paper. He jumped up and
grabbed Graham by the shoulders, staring ferociously down into his son's
terrified eyes. Graham froze. He was petrified. Suddenly Peter turned soft,
pulling Graham close and hugging him.

Meanwhile Mathew continued to loop the island. Nina scooped him
up, delivering him to his seat at the table. "Take off your skates, boys.
Dinner's ready."

"Rollerblades, Mom."

"Take them off!" Nina spooned the spaghetti onto plates and carried
them to the table. "Here's your favorite, gentlemen. I use the term
loosely." She smiled. As soon as their plates hit the table, both boys
grabbed their dinners and exited the room to eat in front of the TV.

"At least we can eat in peace," said Nina.

In the next room, Alex Trebek announced Final Jeopardy. He read
the category, "The Vietnam Conflict," and then went to a commercial.

"I take that back," Nina half joked.

"Dad—you could answer this one. It's about Vietnam!" yelled Graham.

"Nina, I appreciate your letting me go," Peter told her.

"I feel like I'm losing you, Peter . . ."

"Dad!" Graham yelled. "The name of the battle that ended the
French occupation of Vietnam?"

"What if you two are still in love?" Nina asked Peter.

"Dad! The name of the battle that ended the French occupation of
Vietnam?"

"What is Dien Bien Phu?" Peter shouted toward the living room.

"Hey!" Mathew yelled, running to the dining table seeking his mother's protection. As soon as he laid his head in her lap he started to cry. "Graham hit me hard—right in the stomach!"

"I've told Graham not to hit Mathew," Nina looked him in the eyes. "He hits *much too hard.*"

"Don't get me involved." Peter avoided Nina's eyes.

"Don't get you *involved!* You're their *father* for chrissakes!"

"Nina, please. I don't want to get angry."

"Then don't get angry. At least *deal* with it." Nina turned red in the face. "For chrissakes, you're flying off to California to meet your lover from Vietnam . . . and you don't want to get angry! You want to see angry!!" Nina grabbed a piece of garlic bread from the basket and flung it at his face. "I'll show you angry! Goddamn you, Peter!" She lifted Mathew off her lap and stood up. She picked up her plate of uneaten spaghetti and smashed it down on the floor.

"Nina. Don't . . ."

"Why am I doing this for you? Why am I letting you go?" She began to cry.

Peter kneeled beside her chair. Nina leaned against him and he held her head in his hands.

"How can I ever compete with a woman who died for chrissakes— and then *came back* from the dead?"

"Nina, don't . . ."

"You'll probably end up running off with her. I know you will. I can feel it."

Early the next morning, dressed in a windbreaker and jeans, Nina stood beside her husband in the foyer with the front door opened. Peter lifted an overnight bag over his shoulder. "I'll call you from L.A."

Nina gave him a tearful embrace but she couldn't speak.

58

From the outside, the building on Wilshire Boulevard presented a mirrored glass face to the world. *A perfect building for a shrink*, Kate had thought the first time she showed up to see Dr. Sydney Green, Ph.D. But now, years after that first visit, Kate stood inside at the floor-to-ceiling window, transfixed at the sight of the traffic passing silently below through Beverly Hills. Dr. Green leaned back in his comfortable black Eames chair, balancing a clipboard on his knee. Kate hadn't said a word for the past five minutes. She was thinking of the day she had gone swimming in the South China Sea. She tried hard to remember the details—not certain if it had been in Danang or Chu Lai. It was one or the other; she had decided it must've been Chu Lai—yes, it was Chu Lai for sure. At least she thought so, but she wasn't sure. She wasn't sure about anything and it was driving her crazy. She turned to Sydney, remembering she was in the middle of her very expensive therapy session, and told him she didn't think the sessions were doing her any good. "I still can't put a lot of things together," she spoke over her shoulder. "It's so fucking frustrating! During my years at UPI I could remember anything. I could hold five different story scenarios in my mind at once. Now I can't string together one solitary set of events. I'm fucked! So what's the use in my coming here, Sydney?"

She turned to face Sydney, realizing that she towered over him. He looked so small, so meek in his chair with an effeminate way of balancing his clipboard on top of his bony knee. He looked up at Kate with awe in his eyes. Sydney didn't come across women like Kate often—women as strong, self-determined, and beautiful all at the same time.

Kate relished the power she held over Sydney. Kate felt strong in his presence because he seemed so small and frail to her. Besides, she felt Sydney's lust, which made her feel stronger still. Especially since she knew he would never dare to act it out. After all, Kate had shared so many intimate details of her life with him, including stories of the men she had seduced and the ones who had seduced her. Besides, all of them had been warriors in the truest sense of the word, including the young correspondent she'd slept with only a few times but who had remained living in her head all the years since. Her sexuality had always been Kate's refuge. For her, sex was the same as alcohol was for others—it was her solace, her addiction.

Knowing that men still desired her saved Kate from sinking into despair. She swung her hips around and headed for the couch where she flopped down resolutely, flipping her sandals onto the carpet the moment she landed.

"Chlorine," is what she thought she heard Sydney say in his squeaky high-pitched L.A.voice.

"What?"

"Choline, I said. Choline."

"Choline?" She leaned her head on the back of the couch so Sydney came into view.

"You can buy it at the health food store. It's good for the memory—it makes the mind sharper. I know you'll be skeptical but it actually works. I use it myself."

"Thanks for the suggestion." Kate flashed him her fake put-on smile.

"Do you remember anything more about the story you had been working on when you were shot?"

Kate looked up at the ceiling. She lifted her right leg pointing her toe at the ceiling light directly above her. It was a show-offy kind of move, as if she was proving to Sydney what good shape she was in. There was a tear in the leg of her jeans just above her right knee. She had caught Sydney looking there before—more than once.

She answered once she had lowered her leg and rested her foot back down on the couch once again, "The story had been writing itself on so many different levels." She looked over at him, frowning this time. "Sometimes I think the reason I was shot was to blast that stupid story out of my head."

"That's interesting. That's very interesting," said Sydney, sounding enthusiastic for the first time in weeks. "Go on."

"Well, it was getting so goddamn complicated. And, the weird part is that I was becoming part of the story. I was one of the players in the play."

"Well, isn't that why Broward shot you? Precisely because you were an important player—a player who knew too much."

"You're not getting what I'm saying, Sydney."

"Enlighten me, please."

"You're seeing it only on the most basic level. Yes, I was one of the players—that's obvious. But let me see if I can explain. It was like this: First there was that level, the obvious factual one. Then there was what was going on in terms of deception. A second level. So what appeared to be the facts were only the facts because that's the way Broward and Morgan and Tau were manipulating them. They were *creating* the facts. Then there was another level—Broward manipulating Morgan and Tau. Or, you might call it, Broward manipulating the system. Because Morgan ran the system. But Broward *was* the system. Then there was an even deeper level—which was the war itself. Think about it. What was running the war? What was the engine of the war? That was something bigger than any one person. Bigger than governments even. It was some sort of otherworldly force of nature."

"Mmmmh. What exactly . . ."

"A spiritual woman I met after the war—a psychic—told me that Vietnam was filled with demons. This woman felt that it was these demons that were really running the war. She said that explained why the country had been invaded not only by the French but by the Japanese and the Chinese before them!"

"Did you believe her?" Sydney asked.

"It sure explained a lot of things." Kate turned her head toward him to see his expression. "No, not really. I don't really believe that."

"Nor do I," smiled Sydney. "It's too convenient."

"That's the right word, Syd." Kate laughed.

"But I'd like you to tell me, Kate . . . why you think you were there . . . amongst your cast of characters, what was *your* role."

Sydney was losing her. Kate suddenly bolted upright. She planted her bare feet firmly on the carpet and stood up. She looked at Sydney, whose jaw had dropped.

Kate began, "Do you want to know why I've been coming to you, Sydney? Do you want to know the one thing I've been trying to tell you—that I've always been afraid to? I think that now, after all these years, after all this money I've spent—to be perfectly honest—I think it's time I told you." She looked down at Sydney. He seemed smaller than ever, looking like he had sunk part of the way into the expensive leather of his chair.

"Sydney"—Kate's voice cracked—"I don't know how to say this other than to just say it . . ." She felt her knees going weak, so she sat back down on the couch. "When I was ten years old, I was raped . . ." she paused, staring down at her toes on the carpet. "When I was eleven years old, I was raped. When I was twelve and thirteen and . . . I was raped."

Sydney waited for the tears. They didn't come. Instead, Kate continued.

"When I was fourteen, I killed the boy who had been raping me. It was my cousin. I pushed him out of a hayloft just before he was about to do it again. He fell on his head and broke his neck. That's it." She looked Sydney in the eyes. "Can I go now? Am I done?"

59

Peter drove a red Ford Taurus rental car about ten miles per hour along Olive Street in sunny Santa Barbara, California. It was a shaded, tree-lined, wide street that curved through a middle-class neighborhood full of well-kept houses and well-groomed yards. It was the kind of neighborhood where Spanish-speaking men came from poorer towns, somewhere far away, to cut grass and rake leaves for the white middle-class homeowners. He counted down the numbers on each house on the right side of the street—1140, 1138, 1134, until he spotted 1132, the number he was looking for, set in brass numerals on the stucco wall of a two-story white Spanish-style house. It seemed as if Peter was seeing the California version of his own house and neighborhood in Connecticut. He pulled up to the curb and sat for a minute taking it all in. He was more nervous than he thought he would be. He got out of the car, nearly slamming his finger in the door, and headed up the brick walk to the house, hesitating with each step. Halfway there, he remembered the bottle of wine he'd left on the car seat. When he went back to retrieve the bottle, it gave him the time to reconsider—whether he should see Kate at all. But he'd come too far to turn back, so he followed his nose for a second time to the front door. The door opened the moment Peter rang the doorbell. Kate had been watching.

Peter wanted to speak but no words came out. Frozen in his tracks, he wondered if he'd be able to move, let alone speak. Kate gently pulled him inside by his sleeve.

She looked not much older and no less beautiful than she did in Vietnam. Peter wanted just to look at her—it felt something like feasting on a meal that he'd been waiting twenty years for—but instead, he turned away, looking distractedly at the photographs hanging in the hallway. One that caught his eye was of a pretty dark-haired girl on a swing.

"My daughter, Pensi. It was taken a few years ago. She was three. She's thirteen now—quite a different story."

"Are there others?" Peter asked, feeling he'd phrased the question stupidly.

"No, just Pensi," Kate said.

His eyes shifted to a picture of Kate with a man sailing in a small boat. "Your husband?"

She nodded.

"Will I get to meet him?"

"He's in San Francisco on business." Then, quickly changing the subject, she asked, "Can I get you something to drink? Why don't we go into the kitchen?" she said nervously, heading there herself. "Please, come," she instructed Peter, thinking he was frozen in place.

Peter walked behind her into a light and airy kitchen painted pure white with a border of stenciled flowers around the top by the ceiling. Not knowing what else to do, Kate opened the door to the refrigerator and pulled out a carton of orange juice. Peter remembered the bottle of wine he was holding. He placed it on the island beside the orange juice.

"Oh, thanks," she said, taking a moment to read the label. A CALIFORNIA CHARDONNAY.

"It seemed appropriate"—he mouthed the line he'd thought of on the plane—"to bring a bottle of California wine back home."

With a steady stream of thoughts swimming in each of their heads, the two of them remained standing awkwardly across the island from one another. Eventually they allowed their eyes to connect and memories began to flood back. Kate's face softened as she stepped out of her role as mother and began to feel for the first time like she was standing in a room alone with Peter. Still, they found it nearly impossible to speak. It seemed that the gap of so many years wouldn't be bridged that easily—there was still too much unresolved.

Finally Kate spoke. "Let's leave here, Peter. Can we find a place to walk? I need to be away from the house."

As they walked out to the rental car, Peter was hyperconscious of every move they made together. When he opened the door for her and her arm brushed against his shirtsleeve, he was ready to jump out of his skin. He wanted to touch her, to hold her in his arms. Instead, he walked around to the driver's side, got in, and started the engine. Then he focused on the simple task of following Kate's directions to the beach. "Turn right," she said, at the bottom of the hill. "Follow the Pacific Coast Highway and we'll find a place to pull off."

They headed north toward San Luis Obispo. After they were beyond the city limits where they could see the mountains, unobstructed, running down to the sea, Peter pulled into a parking lot that was unoccupied except for a single Volkswagen bus, which had curtains covering all its windows. He and Kate stood in the parking lot, feeling uneasy about being alone.

Peter said, "Maybe we should have gone to Starbucks." He thought it might've been easier to be someplace where they would be among people and where they'd overhear the conversations of others instead of just their own awkward voices.

He took Kate's hand. It felt strange, after so many years, to be holding hands. Kate led him to a winding path that circled back and forth down a steep cliff that ended on the beach. When they reached the sand, Kate took her hand back, stopping to take off her shoes.

"Let's walk here. I don't want to go any closer to the water—the ocean scares me."

When they continued along the beach Peter did not take her hand again. Neither of them was happy. The place was charged with nature's rough energy—with angry-sounding waves, which seemed to be clawing at them as they crashed on the sand. Walking along the ocean brought back their time together in Vietnam. But instead of feeling happy, he walked with his head down as if he were facing into a storm. Looking out across the stormy ocean, Kate was the one to break the silence. Peter sensed the anger sitting just under the surface of her voice. The sound of the breaking waves was so loud that when they finally spoke, they were forced to yell.

"You had no idea I might still be alive?" Kate asked.

He let his thoughts catch up. "I was in the hospital. Nobody had any information about you at all. I thought you were dead."

They stopped and looked blankly out at the misty horizon. "The last thing I remember was your head on the ground in a pool of blood . . . a head wound—nobody survives a head wound."

"You didn't try to find out?"

"I did. I called your bureau from the hospital. No Kate. All they knew was a body had been shipped to Australia." He looked over at her. "Then I went AWOL, for chrissakes. Think how I felt—one minute I was in love, the next, her body's been shipped to fucking Australia!"

Kate's eyes drilled into Peter's. He watched her anger begin to surface but he wasn't prepared when she suddenly slapped him across the face.

Kate stared into his eye, screaming. "You turned out to be the bastard. You were worse than Jake."

"Appreciate the constructive criticism, ma'am."

"You—asshole!"

Kate tried to slap him again but his time he grabbed her hand and threw her down onto the sand. He dived on her before she could get up. She rolled to the side and pushed herself back up to her knees.

"You left me!" she screamed.

She picked up a rock and hurled it at his face. Peter didn't see it coming, and it hit him hard on the side of his head. He reeled and was forced to lie back on the sand. Blood poured down the side of his face. Kate kneeled over him. Peter looked up at her. "Why the fuck didn't you ever call me? *You're* the bastard. At least you knew *I* was alive. You never called!"

"I did—years ago," she admitted. "And I hung up."

"That's a lame excuse—you hung up?"

"One of your kids answered. What difference would it have made anyway—you thought I was dead. If you heard me on the phone you probably would've thought it was a joke, a voice from the dead."

They stared at one another—trying to sort this out.

"How could I know that you even cared about me, for chrissakes? You never said anything. You fucked just about every soldier in Nam."

She tried to kick him again. He grabbed her leg. She fell and Peter jumped on top of her and held her arms to the sides.

"You bastard!" Kate struggled wildly to free herself from his grip but Peter kept a tight hold on her arms.

"Let go of me!" She screamed as loud as she could. But her screams fell mute, muffled by the sand and the roar of the waves.

As soon as she stopped struggling, he let go. Although her arms were free, she didn't try to strike out. She looked as if she'd been shot through the heart.

He saw how hurt she was but he remained straddling her—not ready to trust that she wouldn't lash out again. "I'm sorry . . . I didn't mean to say that."

Kate replied softly, "Yes, you did. You've waited twenty-five years."

"I thought about you so much. After a while I had to forget. You meant too much to me."

Kate looked Peter in the eye. Then she wiped the blood from his forehead with the sleeve of her windbreaker.

However painful their fight was, there was no way around it. They were closing the wounds of twenty-five years gone by—twenty-five years of being lost from each other.

"It's so crazy—after all this time of thinking you were dead . . ."

Kate stopped him. "Peter, I'm alive and . . . time has nothing to do with it."

She lifted her head and blew softly on his wound. Peter turned to face the waves. Exhausted, Kate rolled over and laid her head in his lap. He held her head, running his fingers through her short hair. He wanted to touch her wound and when he did she closed her eyes and started to cry. Then they were silent for a long time looking out to sea.

"Remember when we drove in the jeep—through the rain—out to LZ Danger?"

"You fired at the sniper."

"You were so protective."

"I was amazed that you could fire an M-16."

"We made love afterward in your hootch."

"I thought we just kissed."

"We made love."

"I remember we tried to make the war stop for a while . . ."

"You were so innocent—like a schoolboy."

"Me?"

"I thought it was your first time."

"What?"

"It was the best I've ever had," she went on.

He smiled.

They watched the waves break on the shore when from the far end of the beach a man appeared. He walked with a strange and strong presence along the edge of the water. He was a shadowy figure, his image veiled in the morning mist that covered the beach like a blanket. As the man came closer, it seemed there was something important about him. It was as if he might be the carrier of a message with some significance for them. At first they were not sure what that could be. Although he wasn't an old man, he walked with a slight limp. He had an inner strength, an inexplicable dignity though he wore the tattered

clothes of a homeless man. He carried a beautiful, hand-carved ma-
hogany walking stick tipped with gold. He carried it with aplomb, the
stick obviously his pride, his prized possession.

From their vantage point, the man walked along from right to left at
the edge of the ocean as if he was protected by some timeless knowledge.
He seemed as self-sufficient as anyone could be.

As he approached the space between where they sat and the ocean,
Peter noticed the Montagnard bracelets on his wrists. As close as the
man was at that point, he appeared to be oblivious to their presence.

Or was he? Peter and Kate froze as the man stopped and turned in
front of them. A chill ran up their spines.

He stood completely still, like an animal of the jungle. First he
looked down at the sand as if to gather his thoughts. Then in an art-
ful, inborn motion, he lifted the walking stick and aimed it at point-
blank range between their eyes. He aimed first at Peter, then Kate. It
was the aim of a highly trained marksman, a sniper. The man proved
that he still could've had the kills if he'd wanted. He smiled an eerie
smile and continued on his way along the beach.

They were shaken. Their eyes never left the man as he continued
walking toward the rocks at the end of the beach.

The moment before he disappeared behind the rocks, he looked back
at them one last time, flashing his eerie smile.

60

Kate stood beside Peter on the tarmac in front of a small terminal building at the Santa Barbara Airport. His carry-on bag rested on the ground beside his feet. They were both lost in a sea of thoughts as they looked out across the airfield.

In front of them, passengers were boarding a small regional aircraft about to depart for Los Angeles.

Suddenly and without warning from behind the terminal building, a Huey helicopter roared overhead, its prop wash nearly blowing them over. The sound, echoing off the building, was deafening. There, clearly visible in the pilot's seat, was the man who'd walked along the beach, the same red cap on his head, smiling the same eerie smile. Before heading toward the mountains to the east, Peter saw him wink through his open window. On the white door below the window the word RESCUE was painted in bright red letters. For a few seconds the image of the chopper seemed to fill the sky completely. Kate and Peter watched until it disappeared over the mountains to the east and the air around them settled back down.

"*Strange* is something that follows you and me around," Peter said to Kate.

"Never a dull moment," Kate said. But she'd been thinking of something else. "Peter, I wonder if you and I are still the same people we were during the war."

"How could we be?"

"But what if we don't like these new people—the ones we are now?"

"Can we go back?"

Kate smiled, "Sometimes I've wanted to."

"I know."

"It's never been as good."

"We want to live it again."

"Yeah." Peter laughed.

All the passengers had boarded. The airline agent signaled them to hurry up. Peter dived deep down inside himself and then came up for air. "Coming here to see you . . . brings me back to life again."

Kate looked at him, unable to steady her gaze. "Yes . . ."

"Seeing you again."

"Yes."

He reached out to take her hand.

She took his hand, lifted it, and placed a tarnished coin in his palm. Peter, astonished, recognized the piaster he'd given Kate in the temple.

She folded his fingers, one by one, over the coin until his hand was closed.

"You kept it? All these years."

Peter wiped away the frown on her forehead then pulled her close in a long embrace.

He picked up his bag and began to walk toward the waiting plane. After a few steps, he stopped and walked back to Kate. Kate's eyes filled with tears. Putting his hands on her shoulders, their eyes locked together.

"Are you coming or not?" the agent called.

Peter dropped his hands to his sides. "It's time to go," he told her as he started toward the plane again.

Kate called after him, "Peter?"

He stopped. "Is there something you want to tell me?"

"Yes—only I'm not ready." She looked at the waiting plane, "This is fucking awful!"

"You're right about that." He stopped and turned around one last time. "Do me a favor—don't hang up when you call," he told her. Then he continued to the steps, flipping the piaster into the air, catching it in the palm of his hand.

61

"Gisella, what if I told you that I made this whole thing up?"

She fidgeted in her chair, rolling some loose strands of hair between her thumb and forefinger.

He could tell she was fairly taken aback. "Well, what do you think I would think?"

"I didn't ask about me. I want to know what you would think . . . honestly, as a person, not a therapist—not my therapist."

"I don't know what I'd think. There are many possibilities. First of all, I do believe you. I believe you implicitly."

"What does that mean, *implicitly*? I've never known what *implicitly* means."

"Without question, without doubt."

"Well, I didn't make it up—any of it."

"I know." She smiled. "Why did you ask me that?"

"Because sometimes that's what it feels like. It feels like I made the whole thing up." Peter smiled a half smile, not really knowing what he was going to say next. "You know those dreams I used to have before I started to see you?"

"Yes."

"This whole thing could've been a dream. I mean, couldn't it have been?"

"I don't think so."

"We know Kate exists. Or did exist. We know she wrote a book . . . What if I never met her?"

"But you did!" Gisella was annoyed but caught herself. "Didn't you?"

"I think so."

"Did you know her?"

"Yes, I knew her."

"That's enough. Case closed."

For some reason, Gisella was becoming quite uncomfortable with this conversation. Peter could hear it in her voice.

"You don't want me to talk about it?"

"No, I didn't say that. I don't want you to doubt yourself, that's all."

"But I do."

"What do you doubt?"

"The whole thing. The entire story. The entire war . . ."

"Like it never happened?"

"Yes, exactly. Like it never happened." He smiled a satisfied smile.

Now Gisella felt she really had reason to be annoyed. "Peter, how can you say that the war never happened? Your best friend was killed. You were with him when it happened."

"Not really. I didn't actually see him get . . ."

"You saw his body, yes? He was dead, yes?"

"Well . . ."

"Did you imagine this?"

"Gisella . . ." He started slowly, quietly. "I know you're going to start thinking I'm crazy if I pursue this . . ."

"Peter, I don't think you are crazy. You are not crazy."

"Well, then, will you let me follow this train of thought?"

"Fine."

"Fine." He mimicked her voice.

She frowned.

"You sound so resigned."

"Go on with what you want to tell me."

"What I want to tell you is that sometimes I think the whole god-damn war was a complete sham!"

"That it never happened?"

"No, it might've happened—or it might've not happened. That's not the question. The question is, I'm not sure I was part of it."

"Peter, you are scaring me a little—I have to tell you."

"Hey, that's pretty good, to be scaring my therapist."

"Scaring me for you . . ."

"Say, that's a concept. You are scared for me? But I'm not scared . . ."

"Confused."

"Yes, confused. Definitely confused, thank you. But that's why I came to you in the first place."

"Okay, that's true. I think there were other reasons as well."

"As well! Why can't you just say *too* like other people?"

"Peter, let's talk about why you're feeling angry."

"Angry? Because, Gisella, I feel like a fucking fraud—I feel this huge doubt."

"About what?"

"The whole thing—the whole fucking thing."

"But not the war?"

"No . . . yes . . . even the war."

"Why do you think that?"

"There you go . . . being the therapist again."

"That's what I am, Peter."

Peter lifted a small bottle of Poland Spring water off the coffee table and took a single swallow then put it back down in the exact spot where he'd picked it up. It was a little game he played.

"Look, Gisella, do you want to hear the end of the story? The part right before I left Vietnam?"

She nodded.

"So, when I got out of the hospital, I went AWOL."

"AWOL?" Gisella uncrossed her legs.

"Absent without leave, for chrissakes!" Peter said angrily.

"Peter, why do you feel the need to yell?"

"I'm sorry. I don't know. I just thought you would know what that meant—AWOL, I mean."

"There's a lot of army terms I don't know . . ."

"I know, I apologize."

"Peter, we only have about five minutes left."

He started to push himself up off the couch. "Do you mind if I leave a little early?"

"Is something the matter?"

"No, I just need to go. I need to be somewhere."

"That's fine."

They stood up and hugged one another as they always did at the end of the sessions. Only this time Peter didn't want to let go. He felt as if he needed her as an anchor—as if some sort of strange storm was going to drag him back into the insanity of the past. Feeling the need to hang on for a few moments, he reached his arms all the way around Gisella's waist but was stopped short when his fingers touched the cold, hard metal of a gun handle in the small of her back. He pulled his hands back in shock. "My God! Gisella—I had no clue!"

Peter pushed back in order to focus on her face. Gisella was visibly embarrassed. She didn't offer an excuse. Instead, she let him talk.

Peter walked back to the couch and sat down again. After a few minutes he spoke, looking down at the floor. "So, you don't trust me— you wear a gun to protect yourself from something horrible I might do?" Finally, he looked up at her. "Gisella, how could you think . . ."

"It's standard procedure, Peter. I wear it all the time."

"So that's supposed to make me feel better? You pack a gun for protection from all the demented vets—of which I'm one."

"You are not demented."

"But can you be sure?" Peter asked.

"I'm sure," she said sincerely.

For whatever reason, Peter chose to believe her. He didn't want to destroy all they had built together. It's just that it had been so very odd, at the same moment he was feeling so close to Gisella, to suddenly touch the cold metal of a pistol.

"What kind is it?" he asked her.

Gisella stalled. She didn't want to say.

"What kind of gun is it? A Glock? Something powerful?"

"It's a Derringer."

Peter let out a laugh. "A *Derringer*? What's a *Derringer* going to do? You think you're going to stop me with a *Derringer*?"

"It makes me feel safe—that's all. I don't intend to kill anybody."

"You need to feel safe, Gisella? What's that all about—do I frighten you?"

"Sometimes I *do* feel frightened," she said.

"Can I see it?"

She waited, then reached around her back and pulled it from its holster and held it out for him. She held it with the end of her fingers as if it was a rotten fish.

"I don't want to hold it," Peter said, as she tried to give it to him. "I just wanted to see it—that's all."

There were two doors in Gisella's office, one from the reception room and one next to the window that led directly outside. Peter turned and opened the door that led outside.

"Peter, wait!" she said to his back. But he didn't wait—he needed to get out of there.

62

Peter turned on the light on the night table beside his bed. He opened his left eye only, in order to look at the clock under the lamp. It was four-thirty. He rolled over to look at Nina, whom he saw sleeping soundly. He was happy that she felt better since he'd come back from California. He rolled back the other way, pushing himself out from under the covers. Tiptoeing down the stairs, he went to his office and turned on the computer in the dark. As soon as the screen lit up, he clicked on the icon to access his email. He was interested in one email only. It was there, waiting—a reply from "kwhite" with a title attached, "the end of the story."

peter—please forgive the lack of capitalization—it's very late and i've had a long day with pensi—here goes the story the way I remember it—broward was using refugees—the ones in the crater. randy found out the trucks belonged to operation broward county. the arvns didn't have enough trucks so broward loaned the trucks to tao who had them painted with arvn insignias. the arvns used the trucks to haul cinnamon— you knew that. one more thing—delta company—they were guarding the road for tao's convoy—between quang ngai and the ho chi minh trail—which is why captain hollowell never got the help he needed i guess we already knew this—i guess between the two of us we knew it all. too bad it was never written—kate

63

He continued to stare into his computer screen until it became a blur, then he pulled his Rolodex closer and thumbed to K. On the first card in the section was written simply KATE with her phone number underneath. He dialed, then while he waited for the ring he listened to the hollow, empty sound that seemed to emphasize the distance between them. When her phone finally rang, it sounded so far off. The sixth ring was cut short by Kate's sleepy voice.

His heart pounded in his chest. Suddenly he wanted to hang up. He was frozen. He couldn't speak.

"Peter?" he heard her say.

After a long pause he spoke. "Kate, I needed to talk to you. I know it's early—I'm sorry. I read your email . . . but I don't think that's what you wanted to tell me . . . I already knew all that stuff."

There was silence on the other end and the hollow sound in between.

"I'm sorry for waking you," he said to fill the void.

"It's okay. I wasn't sleeping all that well anyway."

"Is your husband there?" Peter asked, thinking she might not be able to talk.

"Yes. He's sound asleep. He can't hear."

Peter stopped, needing more time to take it in—the fact that Kate's husband was lying so close to her.

"Take all the time you need, Peter," she said, knowing. "You can even call me back if you like. I can wait. However long it takes."

"You are the only one who will understand . . ."

"Yes, well . . ."

"You will. I know you will. I tried to tell Gisella. I thought that maybe then she'd understand. But I've realized something: I don't need to tell *her*, I need to tell *you*. The others . . . if they haven't been there, they just don't *get* it."

"I know. But, tell me *what?*" she said softly.

Peter imagined her head lying sideways on her pillow, the phone close to her mouth, warmed by her breath.

"When we were there—in Vietnam, in the temple, in the jeep, on the road—-wherever we were . . . this is so hard, Kate."

"I know it is, Peter. I know it is."

"It was love, Kate. Although I never said it, I was in love with you. Do you understand?"

"Yes."

"And . . ."

"I was in love with you, Peter."

"Yes. God—Kate, thank you."

"Please don't thank me."

"Do you know why you wanted it to hurt when we made love?"

"Yes."

"Because that's the way you cheated death."

"I know."

"But this is what I have to tell you. It's about what you told me in the temple—your terrible dark secret. It's time for you to forgive yourself, Kate. Because of what happened to you, you already knew about cheating death. You came to Nam to get what you needed. You had to be in the world's most fucked-up place in order to hide such deep pain. You wanted what happened in Nam to hurt enough to cover up your real hurt. You made me realize that it was the same for me. It came to me on the plane back from California—that's why I needed to be there too. Because I already hurt so much. That's why we related so quickly and why it felt so good."

There was no sound on the phone for a long time. Then Peter heard Kate cry. It made him feel helpless and far away. He wanted to put his arms around her but couldn't. He listened to loud sobs, one right after the other, pouring directly out of her heart. They were like the monsoon rain, he thought—her sobs just kept coming in waves as if they would never stop.

"God, my pillow's soaked," she complained when she stopped crying. "Peter, you are so special to me. You know, there's one thing I've been thinking about since you were here."

"What, love?" Peter said, with a lightness in his heart he hadn't felt since he was a child.

"You know that guy who walked up to us on the beach?" Kate asked.

"Hmmm?"

"Who was he?"

"He was it!" Peter said.

"Death, you mean?"

"Just a reminder . . ."

". . . so we wouldn't forget."

After they hung up, Peter remained at his desk staring out the window. He leaned back in his chair feeling sick in the pit of his stomach from the waves of emotion running through him. Behind the trees on the hill, the sky had turned a bright and beautiful cerulean blue.

It was as if he waited for it to happen—as if he knew it would. The phone rang. When he picked it up, he heard Kate's voice sounding clear and awake. "Peter, do something for me . . . no, for both of us. Write this down. I want you to tell this story—it's quite incredible."

Through love alone do hatreds cease.

—Gautama Buddha